CAMPFIRE

CARNAGE

Josh K. Stevens

To My Fellow Campers from so many Moon ago.
Though we haven't talked in ages,
You were the inspiration for this story.
Thankfully, that excursion didn't end the same way this one did.

And to Katie
Even though you refuse to go camping with me,
I'm appreciative that you're my moon and my stars and are
willing to stay on this adventure with me
And thankful that you gave me two kids who are willing to
venture off into the woods from time to time.

Every word I write is for you three.
Even the bad ones.

The Arrival

"Put on a happy face. We're getting out of the car."

The tone of Mindy's voice was irritatingly passive aggressive that Jonas thought he was going to grind his teeth down to dust. He opened his mouth to say something snarky to her but she was already slamming the driver's side door behind her. He closed his eyes and took a deep breath.

I wonder how long it would take me to walk home?

He glanced down at his watch and realized that it had taken just over three hours to make the drive to the middle of nowhere in some sort of Godforsaken Wisconsin wasteland. Considering that he had absolutely no idea where he was in proximity to the comfort of his studio apartment, he decided to forgo any further attempts at calculation. Walking home wasn't in the cards. He would just have to grin and bear it through the long weekend. The long, long weekend. The weekend with no end. Jonas repeated the words in his mind.

Grin and bear it.

I like that.

Maybe I'll use that as a mantra for the next 48 hours.

Grin and fucking bear it.

Oh yeah. That's even better.

With his mantra settled and playing on repeat in his mind, Jonas set his jaw, tossing on a makeshift smile, and opened the car door as he fished a cigarette from his shirt pocket.

Outside the car he was met with a soggy, wet heat that did nothing to assist his mood. He took one step away from the car and then, rethinking his plan, opted instead to lean against the gas guzzling SUV that Mindy had insisted on buying. He fired up his cigarette, breathing in the fresh nicotine, and his eyes scanned the dingy Northern Wisconsin gas station that he had been informed was the "last stop before the wilderness."

His mind wandered back to the last time he had been camping. It had been a ridiculously dry summer when he had set forth into the great wide open with his family. He recalled that drought warnings had peppered the radio and television news for days. Not that he had been actively paying attention, of course, but he had caught enough snippets of the information while flipping through the channels looking for more cartoons. Most of the news coverage had been news anchors recapping which cities had enforced bans on watering lawns during certain hours of the day. Jonas vividly recalled that the corn, which was always cited as having to be knee high by the fourth of July, had barely sprouted to ankle length by the middle of that horrendous summer.

Even though there had been the most miniscule amount of rain since April of that year, five minutes after Jonas' family had pulled into their campsite, the skies had opened up and let loose a torrential downpour that lasted for the five consecutive days that the Reilly family had been scheduled to live off the land. That's not to say that it rained for the entire duration of what was supposed to be a nice, relaxing jaunt into the great outdoors. It had stopped, every afternoon, for a brief four or five hour block during the most unyieldingly scorching portion of the July afternoons, which had allowed for some torturous and muddy hiking excursions through the brutal Wisconsin wilderness where, because of the sudden and unrelenting wet weather, the baseball-sized mosquitos had erupted to life in mass quantities. Jonas had PTSD flashbacks of the memories of trying to breathe the sponge-like air as his father made him traipse through the obscenely damp, oppressively hot woods. He hadn't particularly enjoyed himself in the least to begin with and the hikes were made even worse when he had to spend the majority of the walk trying to swat the winged, blood thirsty devil spawn that were buzzing around his head constantly. He would knock one away and two more of the enormous bastards would take its place. Finally giving up, he had pulled his shirt up over his head and bolted through the jungle and back to camp in search of some sort of relief in the soaked, undrying tent as though he were trying to escape from the Vietcong. Then, as soon as dusk started to settle in, the clouds would roll their way back overhead, and the rain would pour from the sky once again. So as not to succumb to death by drowning, the Reilly family had spent every night restlessly attempting to sleep in their rickety conversion van, which felt something akin to trying to get some shuteye while laying in an oven.

That had all taken place when Jonas was eight. He hadn't been camping since.

Maybe it was the recollection of the genetically enhanced mosquitos or the memories of the sopping wet sleeping bags as the Reilly family had tried to pack up their belongings on that last day of camping when tensions were at an all-time high, but Jonas, now pushing thirty, had been feeling the knot in his stomach tightening further with each mile they had passed as they had approached Westfield.

He had spent the majority of the drive through Illinois and into Wisconsin staring straight ahead with the occasional glance out the passenger side window across the barren landscape that surrounded the highway, not saying a word. He had spent the majority of the journey thinking and, no matter where they wandered, all of his thoughts kept coming back to Mindy.

Jonas would've liked to have been able to convince himself that he was going camping for the first time in nearly seventeen years because he needed to relax and get away from the hustle and bustle of city life. He had, for the past several weeks leading up the excursion, been telling himself (and anyone else who would listen) that he was using the camping trip as an excuse to escape civilization so as to allow for some ideas for his new novel to brew. He endlessly repeated that it would be a good way for him to get away from the book for a few days. He also added that it would be a perfect opportunity for him to not have to deal with the stress and responsibilities that came along with being an adult. For a few days he would be one with nature. No work calls, no deadlines, no word counts, no rewrites, and no responsibilities. Just him, his ideas, and the call of the wild.

He doubted that anyone believed him because, even to himself, he knew that it was a line of bullshit.

You're going camping because Mindy wants to go camping.

It's really as simple as that.

Don't sugar coat it with this hippie nonsense about wanting to reconvene with nature.

Jonas looked around the deserted parking lot and realized that his plastered-on smile was being wasted, seeing as how the rest of the group had already piled inside the gas station to use the last flushable toilet they would see all weekend. He pushed himself off of the car and dropped his cigarette butt to the ground, snuffing it out with the toe of his shoe.

I've got my cigarettes, my sanity, and Mindy. What more do I need?

He shook his head, trying to push away the ever-growing list that had commenced to compile in his head, and made his way to the gas station entrance.

The In-Crowd

Jonas was met with the soft tinkling of the bells bouncing on the glass door to the gas station, followed immediately by the cool, coffee and gasoline smelling air that slapped him in the face. Without hesitation, he made a b-line for the booze, skirting any and all conversation with everyone from his party.

If I don't say a single word to any living soul, I don't have to pretend to be chipper.

If I don't talk to them, they won't talk to me, and Mindy won't complain that I was acting like a douchebag.

"You getting Heine?"

God dammit. That didn't last as long as I had hoped.

Jonas didn't answer right away. He stared down at the six pack of green bottles in his hand, taking a few moments to breathe in through his nose and out through his mouth, the way that the yoga instructor on YouTube had taught him. Granted, he didn't believe that the yogi would approve of him picturing himself punching his fist into someone's throat, but Jonas was taking baby steps. He felt his eyes rolling back in his head. He gritted his teeth, smothering the remnants of some sort of snarky comment that was bubbling to he surface. He took one more deep breath and then exhaled completely before turning around to find Ryan looking over his shoulder. Jonas felt the knot in his stomach loosen a little and his body became more at ease.

"Between this and the rum I have in my duffel bag, I think I'm pretty well stocked for the weekend," he said. Ryan nodded his approval.

"What more do you need?" He asked, shrugging his shoulders.

Continuing where I left off just moments ago: running water, a real toilet, warm towels that have the word "Hilton" embroidered on them...

Jonas bit his tongue. He had nothing against Ryan. In fact, from what Jonas could tell, Ryan seemed like a pretty decent guy. Considering that Jonas was a self-proclaimed, card carrying member of the royal order of misanthropes, that meant something. It also didn't hurt that Ryan seemed to be the only other person on this ludicrous trip that wasn't even remotely thrilled about the whole camping experience they were about to be subjected to. Jonas extended his beer to Ryan.

"Do me a favor and hold these for a second," Jonas said, "I'm gonna use the pisser before we fall out."

"Good idea," Ryan said, "Seeing as how we're going to be shitting in a hole for the next 48 hours."

Jonas gave a polite laugh and turned away from Ryan, heading towards the back of the store and the last vestige of humanity. As he strode towards the bathroom, he glanced around the room at the mishmash of people who were soon to be his camping cohorts. Over in the candy aisle he spotted Mary Beth, her girth impossible to miss, deciding which chocolate treat she was going to annihilate. He noticed that she was holding a Toblerone in her left hand.

11

Ugh… Even her choice in candy is pretentious.

He really didn't care for Mary Beth. He felt a little guilty about his hatred of her. After all, she was nice enough and had never been outright nasty to Jonas, if you could overlook the fact that she was, at heart, an obnoxious know-it-all who tried overly hard to be "divergent". Jonas pushed the guilt aside and mentally shrugged his shoulders.

Really, if you can't make fun of hipsters, who can you make fun of?

Just beyond MB, standing at the counter, Chris and Narissa were purchasing their supplies. It was clear that the store clerk had immediately regretted his decision to ask Chris "How's it goin'?" as it looked like he was presently contemplating hanging himself with his own belt. Jonas laughed, absolutely certain that Chris was yammering on about something that he knew very little and that everyone else didn't care about. Considering that Jonas was well aware that Chris was going to be so overflowing with reminiscences and stories of previous camping excitement that he felt needed to be regaled to everyone present, Jonas was just happy to be away from the vocal diarrhea Chris had been cursed with.

The clerk should just be happy that they don't have to hear stories about Doug.

Ugh… Doug.

Just before he turned the corner to enter the bathroom, Jonas caught sight of Mindy. Both his teeth and his fists clenched. She was standing next to Garrett.

Aside from the actual idea of camping, it was Garrett's presence that was creating the vast itching, burning sensation that was laying just behind Jonas' eyeballs. Garrett. With his muddied jeep and his outdoorsman appeal. Garret, with his redneck wisdom that Jonas could barely understand, which consisted of some jumbled together vomit of consonants and a lack of vowels. It was Garrett that was the root cause of Jonas' irritation.

Just a few weeks previous, Garrett had asked Mindy to be his date to some white trash wedding. Mindy, not wanting to disappoint her old crony, had gladly accepted, leaving Jonas to sit home alone stewing all weekend. He had wanted very badly to crash the wedding and act completely belligerent. Jonas and Mindy had gotten into one of their biggest fights over this issue. Jonas, of course, had apologized for acting like a child and had spent the next week sulking around and doing whatever Mindy had asked as penance. Then, just when Jonas had finally settled down, Garrett had called Mindy in the middle of the night, wasted out of his fucking mind, because he was too drunk to drive home.

It's really too bad he didn't just drive real fast.

Mindy looked away from Garrett and her eyes caught Jonas'. Jonas quickly slipped into the bathroom before she could shoot him another one of her patented "you better be on your best fucking behavior" looks.

The Underlying Situation at Hand

Closing the door behind him, Jonas breathed a sigh of relief.

At least, while in the moderately unsanitary bathroom, he was in his own world. With the wooden door closed, the rag-tag group of campers in the gas station were a world away as far as he was concerned. He stepped up to the urinal, unzipped his pants and closed his eyes, listening to the sound of piss on porcelain. It was a sound that he suddenly realized he too often took for granted. He would surely miss it during the three days in the woods.

This is going to be one hell of a weekend.

You can say that again.

Especially since Garrett is here.

Mindy and Jonas had quite the row whenever Garrett's number lit up her cell phone screen. In fact, it had been more of a set of rows. Each one was worse than the last, but they had all wound up with the same conclusion. After all of the heated words being tossed back and forth, each argument would wind up with Mindy telling Jonas that he "just had to trust her" and Jonas tucking his tail between his legs in order to appease. Jonas didn't have any issues with the actual act of arguing with Mindy. That was a given seeing as how the fights were always lurking in the shadows, waiting for the next time Garrett would call. And Jonas knew that there was always going to be a next time. However, it wasn't the arguments that were the problem. The arguments were never the problem.

In fact, deep down in his heart, Jonas was even able to recognize that Garrett, as an individual, though he was, at best, completely irritating, wasn't even the problem. Jonas didn't even feel particularly threatened by Garrett himself. In fact, Jonas was well aware that, had Mindy opted to take her relationship with Garrett to the next level, he would have no qualms about washing his hands clean of the whole relationship altogether.

Any asshole can see that she'd be trading down if she went for Garrett.

Even I can see that.

At the end of the day, what Jonas shied away from wasn't Mindy leaving him for Garrett. It was Mindy leaving him, period. He just didn't have the stomach to finish a fight that could potentially end with him receiving a swift, hard, kick to the curb. He knew that, if there was ever going to be a potential denouement to his relationship with Mindy, it would be because of one of these particular fights about her involvement with Garrett.

Because Garrett was Doug's best friend.

Garrett and Doug were pretty much joined at the hip which, incidentally, was a location that had previously been held by Mindy. The two had been together for nearly a decade, from Mindy's senior year in high school on and the two had been inseparable. Jonas had only had the pleasure of meeting Doug twice during that ten year span, the same ten year span that he had spent pining after Mindy. Even so, he knew that Doug was an asshole and, therefore, Garrett was also an asshole. A classic case of guilt by association if Jonas had ever seen one.

Jonas knew that, on more than one occasion, Garrett had called Mindy, drunkenly, of course, to try to get her to go out drinking with her old gang. A band of miscreants who had always looked to Doug and Mindy as their regal leaders. Jonas had a feeling that, if Garrett hadn't been borderline mentally handicapped, these calls may have been his clever way of attempting to have Doug and Mindy put their differences aside in order to regain their thrones as the king and queen of whatever trailer park the two would reside in after their shotgun wedding.

Though she would deny it up and down, it was obvious to Jonas that Mindy still had some unresolved feelings for Doug. If Jonas didn't think the feelings were still burning away, then the whole ordeal would've been null and void. Jonas felt that, if Doug wasn't in the picture, then Mindy would have no issues loving Jonas to the same extent that Jonas loved her.

But it all comes down to trust, man.

You gotta have the trust to have real love.

Jonas shook his head. No one could deny the fact that Jonas loved Mindy wholly. It was on display whether he wanted it to be or not. Unfortunately for her, the last time he truly trusted someone, he had his heart launched into the deep black void of space. It was true that, as that old song said, the first cut was, in fact, the deepest. Unfortunately, in Jonas' case, that first cut had been so unreasonably deep that it had completely lacerated any

16

chance of him ever placing that much trust in another human being again.

Fool me once, shame on you… and everyone else who wants to play that game.

Jonas shook the excess drops off and then stood before the urinal for an addition minute. He never would've assumed that he would want to stay in a filthy gas station bathroom for an extended amount of time but, at this juncture, he would've been happy to spend the remainder of the weekend standing in this exact spot. He knew full well, however, that this was an impossibility so he resigned himself to zipping his fly and flushing the urinal. He turned towards the sink to wash his hands under the last bit of running water he would see for a while.

I'll miss you so much it'll hurt.

The sound of the water from the faucet was enough to bring a tear to his eye. He looked away from it and decided that, in order to make this easier, the only logical way to do it was to use the good, old-fashioned band-aid method. He turned the faucet off and reached for a paper towel from the holder. Quick and painless.

If we're using clichés, let's call a spade a spade.

This is more of an "out of the pan and into the fire" moments, isn't it?

Let's face facts: You're not exactly Doug.

And just like that, it all came back to Doug.

He knew that, the moment he walked out that door, he was going to be back in Doug's world. Granted, no one was going to say that outright, but Jonas knew that being "outdoorsy" wasn't his thing. It had been Doug's thing. Even if he tried, Jonas couldn't take that away from him. He would have to erase the very essence of Doug. This was and would always be Doug's territory. No matter how hard he tried, there was no way for him to change that.

He pictured the scene at the campground. The same scene that kept coming back to him over and over again: Everyone sitting around the roaring campfire, beers in hands, regaling each other with story after story, each one better than the last, about all the fun and exciting things that had happened during previous camping excursions with Doug, king of the wild frontier.

It'll get Mindy thinking.

Thinking about the old times. About how much fun she used to have when she had been the queen on the redneck throne. How manly he had been with his grizzly mountain hair and his power to start an ATV with nothing but a mere glance in its general direction. It wasn't even a competition over who was mother nature's true son. Jonas didn't even have a chance. He would lose, had already lost, hands down, no questions asked. If Doug was the wilderness' answer to Arthur Fonzarelli, Jonas would've been lucky to have even been considered as Potsy.

And Mindy is so outdoorsy she's almost feral.

Jonas wished he lived in a Doug free world. He wished that he had the power just to blink his eyes and snuff out Doug's very existence. If every road leading to and from any memories of Doug just vanished, without a trace, then this weekend may have

18

been something that Jonas could've looked forward to. Jonas sighed. That just wasn't in the cards. He had this sinking feeling in his gut that all it was going to take was this one weekend of camping to send Mindy straight back into Doug's strong, tanned, lumberjack like arms. Especially if Jonas saw a spider. He may as well just grab his backpack out of Mindy's car and hitchhike his way home right now.

In all fairness, I bet the spiders up here are the size of human babies.

That doesn't help.

True. I bet Doug never minded though.

Honestly, what do I have to offer?

I work all the time but I have no money.

I write all the time but I can't get this book of the ground.

I've been busting my ass for God only knows how long.

Seven years, three months, twenty-six days, and some change… But who's counting?

I'm possessive, I'm moody, I'm overbearing…

And, to top it all off, you can't even make a fire by rubbing two sticks together.

"I have to get this book done," Jonas mumbled, once again trying his smile on for size. He grabbed the door handle and took a deep breath, "But for the time being, I just need to survive this weekend."

Easier said than done.

Cal

Cal was waiting on the other side of the door, dancing from foot to foot like a marionette, waiting to use the facilities. Jonas waved him in as he walked past.

"It's all yours."

"Thanks, dude," Cal said quickly, "I have to piss like a racehorse."

"Good to know."

Cal was Whitney's cousin and something of an unexpected treat on the camping expedition. He had shown up on Whitney's doorstep that morning, unannounced, as Whitney was walking out of the house. In fact, Whitney had opened the door and was walking out to get in the car when she had literally run into him. After a brief hello and a single-serving of catching up in which Cal had explained that his mother and father had gone to Cancun for the weekend, she had started again towards the car. Just as she was slipping behind the wheel, she had turned back to see the look of disappointment on Cal's face. He had always been her favorite cousin and she felt bad about leaving a him high and dry to hang out with her parents all weekend. She knew that, as exciting as it sounded, sitting on the couch between his Aunt and Uncle watching Blue Bloods on CBS was not exactly how a standard high schooler wanted to spend his Saturday night. She popped back out of the car and, on a whim, had invited him along.

That had been fine to Jonas. It wasn't like he needed someone to hold his hand all weekend. He was a high schooler and, if he was old enough to be left alone while his parents traipsed around Cancun, he was old enough to fend for himself in the wilderness without having to have a babysitter. Besides, apart from bearing a striking resemblance to Ridgemont's very own Jeff Spicoli, Cal had seemed like a pretty nice kid. Everyone seemed pretty content with having the kid around, though, after a ten minute conversation with him, Jonas did have the feeling that the novelty of having Cal along for the ride was going to get real old, real quick.

This kid asks way too many fucking questions.

Jonas was making a mental tick mark on a chalkboard in his mind, thinking that he had just won this round thanks to Cal's obviously filled bladder. Unfortunately, no sooner had the chalk touched the board before Cal poked his head out from the closing bathroom door.

"Hey, I was reading that book about that Ed guy on the way up here," Cal said. Jonas closed his eyes and moved the mark to Cal's side of the board. He turned around to find Cal, half in and half out of the bathroom, still swaying from foot to foot, "Do you think we'll be able to swing by his house?"

"I have no idea," Jonas said, with just the right amount of snip in his voice. Cal nodded and then quickly disappeared back into the bathroom. Jonas shook his head and turned back towards the convenience store.

Jonas couldn't blame Cal for his morbid curiosity. He had been equally as interested when, after doing a bit of research about Westfield, Wisconsin, he had found out that, about twenty miles north of the campground, sat Plainfield, Wisconsin, home of the late, great, serial killer, Ed Gein. If Jonas was being fully forthcoming, he would've admitted that this was one of the main reasons why he had not been able to back out of this camping trip in the first place. He figured that, with any luck, he would be able to steal Mindy's car for a couple hours and take a short but, hopefully, scenic drive out to check out the home of the infamous killer. When he had ran the plan past Mindy, she had merely scoffed at him.

"It'll be a great way to drum up some ideas for this story idea I have," Jonas had informed her.

"That doesn't make it any less creepy," She had responded. He had taken that as a win. She may have scoffed, but she hadn't told him he couldn't. Besides, if he was truly planning on getting any work done on this story, he was going to have to climb out on a few limbs.

"I'm back for the beer," Jonas said as he came up behind the patiently waiting Ryan. Whitney tapped her wrist.

"It's about time," She said sternly. Jonas cracked a smile. He had always had a soft spot for Whit. She was a firecracker and she was funny as hell. She gave her non-existent watch one final tap before flashing one of her trademark smiles and a wink.

"I apologize, I had to get my fair share of the last of the luxuries," Jonas explained, motioning towards the occupied bathroom, "Running water, air conditioning, four walls and a door… I realized that I happen to like those things a lot more than I thought I did."

"Wait… They're not going to have those things up at the campsite?" Whitney asked.

"Not from what I understand," Jonas replied, "I was under the impression that we're roughin' it."

"Do you think," Whitney said, lowering her voice and looking around the room, "We could take that stuff with us?"

"Take what with us?" Mindy asked, rounding the corner and stepping into the conversation. Whitney extended her arms as wide as she could.

"Everything within these walls," She exclaimed, "Including all utilities."

"Oh, honey," Mindy laughed, playfully shoving Whitney's hands back to their sides, "You're living naturally this weekend."

"I wish naturally meant 'working shower'," Ryan stated. Jonas nodded his agreement as he placed his beer on the counter.

"You and me both."

Campground

"Kiss me," Mindy said as she pulled up to the stop sign. Jonas leaned over the center console and pressed his lips against hers. As he started to move back to the comfort of the passenger seat, she reached out and grabbed his face with one hand, squishing his cheeks together. She tilted his head towards hers, looking him in the eyes, "Are we good?"

We'd be better if we were going anywhere else on the planet.

And we'd be perfect if we weren't fraternizing with your old crew.

For the time being, Jonas was perfectly content in letting Mindy think that it was just Garrett who was rubbing him the wrong way. If he opened his mouth, he would instantly open himself up to the inevitable conversation that was looming just on the horizon: Doug. In particular, the amount of time that was left on the countdown before she wound up meeting up with him to try to clear the air. When that happened, Jonas knew that his time with Mindy was short. Once the two of them got together and started reminiscing about the old times, it would only be a matter of time before one thing lead to another and they would be strolling into the middle of the campground, arm in arm, staring longingly into each other's eyes. At the present time, Jonas did not particularly feel like having an aneurysm. He kept his mouth shut.

You can tell the wise man by the bite marks on his tongue.

"Of courth," Jonas said through his mashed lips, "Hunky dory."

Mindy smiled and pulled his face close enough to kiss him on the tip of his nose before releasing his cheeks and checking the rearview. Jonas glanced over his shoulder, watching the other campers' getting into their cars. Once everyone was accounted for, Mindy turned out of the gas station parking lot and headed down one of the unmarked country backroads. Jonas turned back around in his seat and looked out the passenger window at the passing trees. They drove the next twenty minutes in almost complete silence, Jonas lost in thought, not speaking unless Mindy spoke first. Even when Mindy did speak, Jonas' responses were little more that one word answers or barely audible grunts in lieu of actual sentences. Fortunately, Mindy didn't even seem to notice. She was so excited about the prospect of finally arriving at the campsite that Jonas could almost feel the electrical current emanating off of her. As she turned onto the narrow, grass covered dirt road that Jonas could only assume was leading them closer and closer to the campground, her excitement began to multiply at an infinite pace. She stopped the car when a heavy, metal chain came into view across the road before them and her mood had become just short of giddy.

"Home sweet home," Mindy said, almost singing, as she threw the car in park and jumped out to unhook the chain that was hanging across what Jonas considered the driveway to her family's 48-acre lot. Mindy motioned for Garrett to drive ahead before she got back in the car. Garrett revved the engine of his pick-up truck and pulled around Mindy's car to speed off into the dense forest beyond.

"He needs to drive ahead and check the road," Mindy explained as she climbed back into the driver's seat, "Make sure it's not washed out or anything."

Good to know. I'm glad he wasn't just bolting ahead to start having all sorts of fun without me.

Mindy stared out the driver's side window, longingly taking in the trees around her, before she put the car back in drive. She moved her eyes back to the road in front of her and let out a sigh when she saw that Garrett's truck had already disappeared from view.

"Boys will be boys," She stated wistfully, "He was always all about off-roading."

The men in my family never needed super off-road vehicles... We were born with penises.

As Mindy drove down the path after Garrett, Jonas watched the trees on either side of the road grow thicker and more dense with every inch they travelled. The canopy began to mesh together, creating a dusky tunnel that spread out before them with no end in sight. Jonas felt his chest tighten as he came to the dawning realization that there really was no turning back at this point. He was here and he was going to be here all weekend. He gave a silent sigh of defeat, deciding in that moment that it was best to just take in the surroundings, knuckle down, and do his best to enjoy himself. He reached out and wound down the

26

window, noticing the smaller, dirt paths that lead off from the driveway. He assumed these were for the quads and dirt bikes that Mindy had so often talked about. He stories had made riding them sound fun but, now that he was seeing them in person, he just thought that they looked incredibly dangerous. He made a mental note to avoid riding the hillbilly chariots at all costs. He averted his eyes back to the seemingly endless road ahead, finally seeing a small glimmer of light at the end of the literal tunnel. As they approached, he noticed what appeared to be a rusted, abandoned camper just off the drive.

"This place must be creepy as hell at night," Jonas thought out loud. Mindy nodded her agreement, barely noticing what he had said, as she emerged from the trees and into the tall grass of an open field. Jonas narrowed his eyes against the sudden reemergence into the daylight. He blinked until his eyes adjusted back to the light and then he took a glance around, surveying the accommodations. Ahead of them stood a pole barn, which Mindy pulled the car towards until she was just a few feet away. Off to his left there was a fire pit in the center of a small dirt clearing and, if he squinted his eyes just right, he could make out an outhouse just inside the tree line.

All we need is an inbred mental-case with a banjo.

Mindy threw her car into park and jumped out of the car, extending her arms as wide as she could. With a smile on her face, she looked through the open door and across the car at Jonas.

"We're here!" She yelled. Jonas forced a smile and a laugh. He pushed open his own door and stepped out into the campground.

Like it or not, camping had commenced.

Getting Ready

When it came to setting up camp, Mindy "had a system".

This "system", from what Jonas could tell, more or less entailed Mindy barking orders, telling him what to do with a nearly endless series of tasks that he was supposed to complete immediately. Once Jonas had conditioned himself to tune out her voice, he was pleasantly surprised that that the actual setting up of the campsite was a hell of a lot easier than he had anticipated. Mindy and Jonas had their tent set up well before anyone else had even removed theirs from their vehicles. Jonas stepped back to admire the tent, thinking that he could now spend the rest of the afternoon enjoying himself when Mindy pulled a second tent from the back of her SUV.

"Are we setting up a second tent to show off?" Jonas asked with a quizzical look, "Because I don't really think that's necessary."

"I told Coral that I'd set up a tent for her when we got here.," Mindy informed him, "I told you that in the car."

"That's right," Jonas said, opting not to ask any follow up questions so as to not let on that he hadn't been listening to her for the majority of the car ride up. He had the vaguest recollection that Mindy had, in fact, mentioned something about her roommate would be joining them. He couldn't recall hearing about the roommate's boyfriend. In fact, he didn't even realize Coral had a boyfriend.

He must be a saint if he can put up with her.

She's not that bad.

No. She's much, much worse.

He shrugged it off and set to work assisting Mindy in setting up the second tent. When they were finished, Jonas stood back and admired his handiwork. He had a brief moment in which he thought that maybe he wouldn't mind this rugged lifestyle after all. He clapped his hands together and looked around the field at the other campers. He saw that Mary Beth, sweating profusely and breathing heavily, was almost done setting her tent up. He raised an eyebrow.

I expected her tent to be much larger.

He smiled, in spite of himself, as he imagined the Westfield natives lining up outside the campground, money in their hands and an air of excitement about them, thinking that the circus had come to town.

"Ryan, do you need help?" Mindy called out, pulling Jonas out of his daydream. Jonas glanced behind him at Ryan and Whitney. They were fumbling about, trying to drive stakes into the ground while simultaneously keeping their massive cloth mansion upright.

"Jesus, how many people are staying in your tent?" Jonas asked. Ryan shook his head but didn't look up from the task at hand.

"It looked a lot smaller on the box," He muttered, trying in vain not to let his obvious irritation marinate his words.

He and Mary Beth should trade tents. I mean, after all, she could probably use her current digs as a pair of underwear.

"If you're sure you don't need help, then I'm going to get the trailer unloaded," Mindy called. Ryan waved her away. She shrugged and slapped Jonas on the shoulder, "Fine. Let's get unpack the trailer."

Mindy walked away from the circle of tents and moved towards the trailer that was hitched to the back of her SUV. Jonas took one last look around. Ryan was fully engrossed in his work and, seeing as how Jonas was not yet feeling up to the task of making small talk with anyone else this early in the day, he turned and followed Mindy across the field.

"Where's everything going?" He asked as he approached.

"Coolers by the picnic table," Mindy answered. Her response was short and crisp. Jonas knew, subconsciously, that this was because she was in the zone, but he still found himself trying to find a hidden meaning in her snippy response. As he unfastened the tie downs and heaved one of the coolers off of the trailer, he tried to let the question of whether or not Mindy was still pissed off at him float to the back of his mind.

Let it go. You'll find out soon enough.

"Y'unt th' toys off?"

Jonas rolled his eyes as Garrett's drawl cut in from behind him. He turned around to find that Garrett had come from behind his mud splattered Jeep and was motioning with his cigarette towards the quad and the bike.

"They're certainly not going to do us a whole lot of good if they stay up there," Mindy said, bending down to grab a case of water from the ground. Jonas moved in to take the water from her, using chivalry in a poor attempt at avoiding having to hang around with Garrett. Mindy moved the water out of his reach and cocked her head towards the trailer, "Jonas, why don't you help him get that stuff out of there?"

She's learning my tricks.

Jonas opened his mouth to come up with an excuse as to why he was unable to do so, but he wasn't quick enough to think of something. The bullshit excuse that was rattling around his brain at present wouldn't have been a good one seeing as how it had now been ten seconds and it still wasn't even a full thought. Not that it mattered. Even if he had been prepared with an excuse as to why, though he would love to, he just simply could not assist Garrett in emptying the trailer, Mindy wouldn't have budged. She hadn't even been planning on waiting for an answer. She was already halfway across the field with a case of water. Jonas stared at her ass as she strode away.

It's the little victories… I'm not a proud man.

After a few seconds, Jonas closed his mouth in defeat and turned to face Garrett, who was already busying himself by unhooking the clasps around the bike. Jonas took solace in the fact that this whole ordeal was going to be equally as awkward for Garrett as it was for him. It put him a fraction closer to be at ease. He took a few steps to move closer to the trailer, feeling out of place.

"What do you want me to do?" Jonas asked. Garrett paused, cigarette between his lips, and he slowly raised his head to look

Jonas in the eyes. He thought about it for a second before he shrugged.

"Nu'n ya c'n do righ'naw," Garrett drawled, the cigarette bouncing between his lips, "I s'pose ya c'n hol' 'er stready so's she don't topple ovah." He patted the seat of the bike like it was a big, husky dog before he returned to untying the bikes. Jonas rolled his eyes again and stepped up to the side of the bike, resting his hand on the seat cushion. He didn't particularly feel as though he was helping so much as leaning. At least he was creating the illusion that he was helping. He figured that would go a long way if Mindy happened to be watching.

"Now, we c'n pull'er down an' gassum up," Garrett said as he tossed the tie downs off to the side, "Y'umpta take th' frontch?" Jonas nodded his agreement, though he was not entirely sure what he had agreed to. Garrett pulled the cigarette from his mouth with two fingers and motioned towards the bike's handlebars as he reached for the back of the bike with his free hand. Jonas grabbed the front of the bike and they lifted the bike from the trailer, walking it steadily down, before setting it on the moist grass.

Mindy walked over and Jonas averted his eyes, pretending to be engrossed in the front wheel of the bike so as not to shoot her a dirty look for leaving him alone with Grizzly Adams.

He was certain that Garrett was probably doing the same thing with the rear tire.

"Y'umpta gasser and taker fer a spin?" Garrett drawled to a grinning Mindy. Jonas looked up and cocked an eyebrow.

Apparently he was not as affected by the previous close encounter as I was.

Mindy's grin quickly fizzled out. She closed her eyes and slapped her forehead with the palm of her hand.

"Might help if I had remembered to fill up the gas cans while we were at the gas station," She growled. She shook her head and looked to the opposite side of the campground at the poll barn, "I'll see if there's any gas left over from last year."

"We's git t'oth'r one off," Garrett stated, gesturing at the quad. Jonas gritted his teeth.

Dammit, man. You have to move faster if you want to escape.

Jonas walked back to the front of the trailer, watching Mindy walk away. He reached down and grabbed hold of the front of the four-wheeler just as Garrett took a seat atop it. They looked at one another and it was hard to say whose face was more puzzled.

"Whatcha doin'?" Garrett asked, "We's don' gotta lif' this'n. Jus' unhooker."

Jonas sent up a silent prayer of thanks and pulled the latch as Garrett started the quad. The trailer upended itself and the four-wheeler rolled down the elevated surface and onto the grass. Garrett turned the throttle and took it for a quick spin around the field before parking it in the shade of the poll barn. Mindy poked her head out the door.

"We have a little bit left," She called, "Should be enough to last until morning."

"I'll run into town and fill up the cans after we eat," Jonas piped up as he crossed the field. Mindy narrowed her eyes at him and he quickly added, "I need more cigarettes anyway."

"I thought you brought three packs?" Mindy interrogated.

"I did," Jonas replied, "But I'm already down to two and a half. If I keep smoking at this rate, I'll be completely out by tomorrow evening."

Mindy narrowed her eyes even further. Jonas felt as though he were at a parole board hearing. After what felt like a decade of Mindy mulling over his response, she nodded her approval. Parole was granted. Jonas breathed a sigh of exaltation, though he didn't believe for a second that she had actually believed his song and dance. Mindy began busying herself with prepping the four-wheeler and Jonas quickly walked away before she could change her mind. He lit a cigarette as he walked back to camp.

Ryan was standing beside his tent, admiring his work, arms crossed over his chest and a smile plastered across his face. Jonas stood beside him and took a deep drag off of the cigarette.

"You up for a ride into town in a little while?" He asked. Ryan nodded, never once removing his eyes from the tent. They were filled with pride and joy.

He looks like a kid on Christmas morning.

Jonas looked at Ryan's tent for a few more seconds before he lowered his eyebrows thoughtfully. He slowly looked around at the rest of the tents. Then he returned his attention back to Ryan's.

"Looks good," Jonas said. Ryan nodded his approval. Jonas nodded back. Mindy walked up and stood between them resting an elbow on each of their shoulders as she surveyed the tent before them. Jonas hitched a thumb towards the lodging, "Ryan finished setting up his tent."

"The door is facing the wrong way," Mindy said without hesitation. Ryan took a deep breath. He glanced around at the other tents in the circle then fixed his gaze back on his own tent. Jonas snuck a look and watched as every ounce of pride in Ryan's eyes escaped like victims of a shipwreck. Ryan shook his head.

"If you need it turned around," He stated calmly, "You can feel free to do it your god damned self." With that, he turned and walked towards the fire pit.

Mindy looked at Jonas and, when their eyes met, they couldn't help but laugh.

"So, you're telling me that this guy was the basis for the movie 'Psycho'?"

The hatchet made a sharp "THWACK" as it stuck in the tree trunk. Jonas nodded his head as he strode across the muddy ground in the forest opening.

"And 'The Texas Chainsaw Massacre'," He said as he gripped the handle of the hatchet and yanked the blade free from the tree trunk. He walked back and handed the hatchet to Ryan, "I mean, they were based loosely, of course."

Ryan nodded, mulling it over in his head, as he squared his legs and brought the hatchet up over his shoulder. He stared at the tree trunk and let loose. Jonas watched as the hatchet flew, end over end, across the grove and stuck in the tree trunk again.

THWACK.

"What was it that Gein did exactly?" Ryan asked, admiring his throw.

"He killed people," Jonas shrugged, "He killed several people."

"Well, no shit. He was a serial killer," Ryan said as he pried the hatchet loose, "I mean, what made him famous?"

"His insanity," Jonas said. Ryan extended the hatchet to Jonas. Jonas took it and curled his elbow up.

"Right," Ryan said slowly, "Because, as we all know, serial killers, in general, aren't insane."

"I'm not saying that, smart ass," Jonas retorted, hurling the hatchet through the air, "For Gein, it was all about timing."

THWACK.

"Timing?"

"He was at his peak in the 50s," Jonas explained, walking to the tree again, "He wanted to be a woman and was legitimately considering a sex change but he was afraid to go through with it…"

"I can understand that," Ryan said.

"Also, it cost too much," Jonas continued. Ryan held out his hand to take the hatchet but Jonas held it up and cocked his head, "Keep throwing this or do you want to try tossing the machetes?" Ryan rubbed his chin with his fingers. Then he shook his head.

"My machete is in the car," He said, "I don't feel like walking over there to get it."

"If you change your mind, I've got mine out here," Jonas said, motioning towards the tree stump a few feet behind them. Ryan considered it for a moment longer and then shook his head again.

"Nah," He replied, "I've gotta beat you at this game before I go back to the machete."

"Good luck with that," Jonas mocked. He handed Ryan the hatchet.

"Okay," Ryan said, squaring up to throw, "So, Gein wanted to be a woman and that made him crazy?"

"No," Jonas said, "Well, yeah. It was outside the norm so, technically, it made him ahead of his time. What made him crazy was that, instead of getting the operation, he decided to make a suit so he could be a part-time woman." Ryan threw the hatchet.

"Fuck!" He yelled as the hatched hit the tree and bounced off and into the grass, "God dammit!"

"Eleven to twenty," Jonas said, "My lead."

"How did you get so god damned good at this?" Ryan asked.

"I used to work at a Wild West Town and they had a hatchet throwing station," Jonas said, pulling a cigarette from the pack in his pocket, "When I was assigned the station and it was quiet, I spent a lot of time practicing."

"Sounds rough," Ryan said as he bent to grab the hatchet from the ground.

"It was."

"Okay, Gein made a suit so he could be a lady?" Ryan said, jumping back into the conversation as he handed Jonas the hatchet, "Like, 'Silence of the Lambs' style?"

"Exactly," Jonas said, heaving the hatchet, "Another character based on Ed Gein."

THWACK.

"Did he do it the same way as Buffalo Bill?"

"Eventually he resorted to abduction," Jonas said, "But he started off just robbing graves."

"Fucking gross."

"Totally fucking gross," Jonas agreed, "But the lady-suit wasn't even the grossest thing he made."

THWACK.

"If you try to tell me Frankenstein was based on Gein…" Ryan said, raising an eyebrow.

"No," Jonas said, grabbing the hatchet again, "Gein was more of a carpenter than a mad scientist. He made more… household items."

"Household items?" Ryan asked, "Like what?"

"Bowls out of skull caps, mobiles out of noses and lips, lamp shades, furniture upholstery, and garbage cans out of the skin," Jonas ticked off on his fingers. He raised his arm to throw the hatchet, then paused, "Oh, and he made a belt out of nipples."

THWACK.

"Why the hell would he do that?"

"Who knows?" Jonas said, "Maybe his mother didn't hug him enough as a child."

Ryan nodded sullenly as Jonas passed the hatchet off.

That seems like it may have struck a nerve. You should probably let him know it was a joke.

"Why did he start killing people?"

"No one knows," Jonas admitted, "A deeper need for blood, maybe? Once you start down the crazy trail, it's probably only a matter of time before you spin out of control."

"I can't argue with that logic," Ryan said. He let loose the hatchet again. His throw went wide and sailed past the tree, landing in the weedy underbrush beside the tree line. Ryan clenched his fists, "Son of a bitch."

"Nice throw," Jonas said as he started towards the weeds to find their toy.

"Shut up," Ryan shot back. He walked over to help Jonas sift through the weeds, "How many people did he knock off?"

"He admitted to two," Jonas said, "But there's always been speculation that he killed a lot more."

"Ah HA!" Ryan said, pulling the hatchet from the weeds. Jonas gave him a thumbs up and they started back, "Why'd he confess?"

"He didn't have a choice," Jonas explained, plucking the hatchet from Ryan's hand, "The cops found a body in his shed."

"Maybe he should've hid it better."

"Seeing as how they never found the other body they were looking for, he probably would have," Jonas replied, "He just wasn't done carving her up yet."

THWACK.

"Carving her up?" Ryan asked, making a face that said he wasn't sure if he wanted to hear more.

"Yeah," Jonas went on, "She was hanging from the rafters when they found her. Headless, gutted like a deer. Her 'lady parts' were all cut out."

"Good lord."

"The cops found her heart in a saucepan on the stove, her other organs in a box on his kitchen counter, and her head, with nails in the ears, hanging from some twine in his living room," Jonas rattled off. He glanced at Ryan and saw the look of disgust on his face.

"How do you know this shit?" Ryan asked.

You kind of sound like a lunatic yourself, Jonas, ya' fucking freakshow.

"Read a fucking book once in a while," Jonas laughed.

THWACK.

"What happened to him?"

"He got arrested, confessed to two murders and some robbed graves, got locked in a mental ward," Jonas shrugged, "Nothing exciting."

"Why the hell didn't they fry the bastard?" Ryan asked. Jonas pulled another cigarette from his pocket and, opened his mouth to answer when another voice piped in.

"Judge said he wasn't fit to stand trial."

Ryan and Jonas both wheeled around as Cal stepped from the trees. Cal grinned at them, looking at the look of surprise on their faces.

"Did I scare you guys?"

"I almost whipped this thing at you. Don't sneak up on a guy with an axe," Ryan said, shaking his head, "I think I'm done listening to horror stories for the day."

"That's a hatchet, Ryan. There's a difference," Cal said. He motioned towards the tree behind them, "You guys playing prairie darts? Can I join?"

"Sure," Ryan said, "But we're just about done. It's gonna be dark soon."

As Cal took the hatchet from Ryan, Mindy's voice boomed from back at camp.

"Dinner's on, campers!"

Jonas tucked his unlit cigarette back into this pocket and looked at Cal and Ryan.

"Sorry, gentlemen," He said, "I'm bowing out. There's only so much ass that I can kick on an empty stomach."

"Can I take a rain check?" Ryan said to Cal, "I'm pretty starving myself."

"Totally. I'll getcha tomorrow," Cal said. He turned towards the tree and raised the hatchet to his shoulder, "But I'm going to practice for a little while."

"Fair enough," Ryan said, punching Jonas in the shoulder, "If you're gonna go toe to toe with this guy, you're gonna need it."

"I think I can handle him," Cal said, with all of the bravado that only an eight-foot-tall, bulletproof teenager could manage.

"We'll see you back at camp."

THWACK.

Ride to Town

"Mindy said to follow the curve."

"Do you remember any of this at all?" Whitney asked. Jonas clenched his teeth and opted not to justify her question with a verbal response.

Any part of what? All there is on either side of the road is barren cornfields.

"I certainly don't," Ryan piped up from the back seat. Jonas looked in the rearview mirror and stifled a laugh. There was a small part of him that felt sorry for Ryan, who had been stuck in the backseat with Mary Beth. But, in all fairness, Whitney had followed standard shotgun rules and called "shotgun" with the car in sight and the driver present. Jonas was not about to argue.

Jonas returned his attention to the road. For now, Jonas had to focus on getting them back to town. Mindy had attempted to give him directions, but he wasn't entirely good with directions unless they came from the GPS on his phone and, considering they were in the middle of nowhere and his phone wasn't getting any reception, that was a moot point. Regardless, Jonas had pretended to listen, figuring that it couldn't be that hard to take this quick and easy trek back to civilization. He had also figured that one of the three people who was going with him would have some idea of where to go. Unfortunately, he had been wrong on both counts.

"There's a sign up there," Mary Beth pointed out, roughly tapping Jonas' shoulder, "We're coming to a town."

"Welcome to Harrisburg," Whitney read aloud.

"Harrisburg? Where the fuck is Harrisburg?" Jonas asked, "Did we even drive through a Harrisburg on the way up here?"

"Nope," Ryan answered, "Definitely not. Maybe we should find a gas station and ask for directions." Jonas shook his head, feeling his male machismo kicking into high gear.

"Absolutely not," He said, not even attempting to mask his stubborn streak, "We'll figure this out on our own. After all, we're not idiots."

"Ryan is," Whitney giggled. Jonas smirked.

"Then it's a good thing he's not driving, isn't it?"

"Hey, asshole, you're the one that got us lost as hell," Ryan retorted with more than an air of defense in his voice, "And, by the way, if I was driving, we'd be going a whole hell of a lot faster that you are, grampy." Jonas looked down at the speedometer and his grin faded from his face and was replaced with a scowl. He pressed his foot down heavily on the gas pedal.

"I wouldn't speed up just yet. We may want to turn around," Whitney suggested, tapping her finger against the window, "It doesn't look like there's going to be a gas station in this one-horse town." Jonas glanced out the passenger window at the dilapidated buildings lining the downtown business district.

"I don't even know if this town has one horse," He muttered, "Or anything else for that matter."

Almost ever single building was flanked by an abandoned storefront that looked even worse for wear than the

45

one beside it. One building had actually fallen down completely and, from the looks of it, it had been that way for quite some time. Lying there, where it had once stood erect, no more than the rubble of a memory of its former state.

"This looks like Detroit," Mary Beth said, "And I would remember going through someplace that looks like Detroit. I went there once, when I was in college. Did I ever tell you about it?"

For the love of God, I don't even know what that means or how it applies here.

"You don't remember it because we didn't go through it," Jonas snapped, his irritation level finally reaching its breaking point. Ryan could feel the heightening tension in the car.

"Just find a gas station and I'll get out and ask for directions," He said, trying to keep everyone, mostly Jonas, calm. Whitney pointed out the window again at the dark building on the corner.

"I'm guessing that'll be a lot easier said than done," She said. Jonas slowed the car as he neared the corner to get a better look at the gas station they were passing. He couldn't tell if it was closed or abandoned but, either way, it was definitely not conducive to their current situation. He gave a guttural sigh of anger and slammed his hand on the steering wheel.

"What the hell kind of town closes up shop at nine at night?" He growled. He didn't wait for a response from the passengers before he pulled sharply into the gas station's empty lot, "Fuck this. We'll just turn around."

46

"Maybe Mindy said don't follow the curve," Ryan observed. Jonas nodded.

Thanks, Helpy Helperton.

"That's probably the case," He muttered, "We'll just go back from whence we came and turn down the road that's just before the curve." He gave the wheel a harsh spin and pulled back out on the street.

Dusk had rolled in on them quickly, changing the sky from twilight to black in slowly darkening shades of gray. As Jonas tried to regain his bearings, he glanced down at the speedometer again, noting that he was doing only forty-five, ten miles an hour under the posted speed limit.

If Ryan says one word about how fast I'm driving, I'll make his ass walk back to camp.

At this rate, he'd probably get back there before you do.

All for of the city dwellers were looking out their windows, looking for anything recognizable and trying their damndest to figure out where they were. No one said a word, but it didn't take a psychic to know that they were all thinking the same thing Jonas was.

Where the fuck are we?

After what seemed like an eternity of driving in strained silence, Whitney pointed excitedly out the driver's side window, damn near taking Jonas' nose off in the process.

"Is that the road?"

Jonas slowed the car to a crawling pace as he squinted out the window, trying to make heads or tails out his location.

47

"The road is curving, though," Ryan observed.

"This has got to be it," Jonas said, not entirely sure but holding out hope. He turned the wheel and took the side road.

"I think I remember seeing that sign," Whitney said, this time motioning out her own window. Jonas nodded. He didn't recall shit but he wasn't entirely surprised.

Welcome to Wisconsin, folks. Please enjoy our lack of landmarks and our excess of desolate fields that all look fucking identical.

"Wait a minute," He said, more to himself than to anyone in the car, "I remember those fucking things."

"What things?"

"Those… things. Those… I don't know… Whatever the fuck things. Out in the field," Jonas stammered, rapping his knuckle against the driver's side window, "I don't know what the hell they are. Sprinklers, maybe?" Whitney nodded in agreement.

"I remember them," She said, excitedly, "We're back on track!"

Thank God for small victories. If it weren't for small victories, I'd have…

"Harrisburg Bingo Night," Mary Beth said out of nowhere. Jonas shook his head and shot a quizzical look over his shoulder at her.

"What?"

"That sign back there, on the side of the road, read 'Harrisburg Bingo Night'," She stated, hiking a thumb over her shoulder.

48

She paused for a moment before asking, "Are we back in Harrisburg?"

Jonas shook his head, preparing himself to argue the fact that there was no possible way they could be back in Harrisburg. Then he felt the calm, collected thoughts in his mind fall by the wayside as the car once again rolled past another street sign.

You have got to be fucking kidding me.

"Welcome to Harrisburg," Ryan read, just in case anyone's eyes were deceiving them. Jonas moved his head in a circular motion on his neck, trying to free some of the tension that had been building in his muscles.

"Okay then," He said in a hushed tone that was barely audible to anyone else in the car. He tapped his fingers on the steering wheel, "Apparently, when we followed the curve, we wound up in a goddamn horror story where time and space don't exist."

When four weary travelers from the city find themselves on a desolate road in the middle of the Midwest without a map, they figure it will be easy to return back to town. What they don't realize is that their wrong turn will lead them directly into… The Twilight Zone.

"There are some people on the side of the road," Ryan said, tapping Jonas' shoulder and silencing the voice of Rod Serling in his head, "Pull over and ask them where we are." Jonas leaned forward over the steering column trying to make out the shadows on the shoulder of the road. As the car's headlights washed over them and they came into view, Jonas leaned back and nixed the idea. He put his foot down on the gas.

"What are you doing?" Ryan asked, looking out the back window, "Why didn't you stop and ask for help?"

"Because those girls looked like they've just barely reached the ripe old age of twelve," Jonas scoffed, "If I had pulled over to ask them directions, all they were gonna do was shriek and run away."

"Either that or they would've killed us and disposed of our bodies," Whitney quipped. Jonas looked over at her, unable to hide the look of surprise that registered on his face. Whit looked back and shrugged, "Well, if we were in a horror movie, that's what would've happened."

"Children of the Corn," Ryan said without missing a beat. If Jonas had any second thoughts about driving past the two girls on the side of the road, that was enough to seal the deal. He glanced in his rearview mirror as the two girls, momentarily bathed in the red glow of the taillights, disappeared from view altogether.

They drove on in silence for a few more miles, passing into a completely different part of Harrisburg, but one that was also seemingly abandoned and forgotten. Jonas took a deep breath, preparing to concede defeat and spend the night in the car by the side of the road.

Apparently, I live here now.

"That place has a light on," Mary Beth said, leaning over into the front seat and extending an arm to point through the windshield, "Why don't we stop there and ask someone for directions?"

Jonas slowed the car to a halt on the street in front of the building and peered through the windshield at the faintly glowing sign perched in the window before them.

"Herod's Tavern," Jonas read with a nod. He scanned the parking lot, finding it empty, save for one beat-up pick-up truck with a bumper sticker that read "They call it the White House for a reason" parked haphazardly across two spaces.

An ancient relic of redneck days gone by.

"I know asking for directions was my idea, but this doesn't seem wise," Ryan said, bringing Jonas' thoughts to life, "There's one truck in the lot. I say we keep driving until we find someplace a little less foreboding."

"Guys, we don't really have that many options," Whitney said, motioning up and down the otherwise empty and darkened street. Jonas couldn't help but wonder if she actually thought that they should mosey inside the bar or if she just wanted to argue with Ryan. At this juncture, either notion seemed pretty feasible. Whitney continued, "There's no gas station, there's no stores, convenient or inconvenient, there's no nothing. Either we ask for directions here or we're apt to continue wandering aimlessly through the Wisconsin countryside."

Just like a hillbilly Moses.

That's a great name for a country song.

"She has a point," Jonas agreed, "I'd like to get back to…" He stopped himself, disgusted by the idea that he had been on the verge of finishing that sentence with the word "camp". The truth was, he didn't want to get back to camp. He didn't want to get

51

back to the real world either. He honestly didn't know where he wanted to get back to, he just knew that he wanted to get far away from here. He inched the car forward and pulled into the lot.

Escapism comes in many forms.

This could be a chapter in your next novel.

If you ever finish the first one.

"I'll run in and get directions," He said, unbuckling his seatbelt and feeling his masculinity deflate like a punctured balloon. He put the car in park and reached for the door handle. Mary Beth opened hers as well.

"I'll come with you."

So much for escaping.

Big Fat Mouth

Jonas hadn't been expecting the inside of the bar to be nice, but he was appalled to find that it was actually far worse than he had imagined.

This town clearly does not have a health inspector.

To call this bar a hole in the wall was a disrespect to hole in the wall bars everywhere across the globe. The lighting in the bar was minimal at best, with the back-hanging lightbulb flickering dully, creating a dim atmosphere that was slightly less inviting than a creepy basement. The floor was covered with a potpourri of peanut casings and beer bottle caps, with the occasional wadded up paper towel thrown in for good measure. Jonas was certain that he had also seen at minimum three shotgun shells and a used condom.

This place looks like it hasn't been cleaned since the Reagan administration.

Even that might be too generous.

If you looked around some, I betcha you could find a Billy Beer tab.

The walls of the joint were covered in what could only be described as "white trash décor." Mounted stag heads with Christmas lights tangled in their antlers, neon beer signs with half-naked cartoon women, rusted metal street signs, and, interspersed between all of this "art", was the occasional out of place humorous sign that made absolutely no sense when viewed out of context. ("Welcome to our ool... Notice there's no P in it. Please keep it that way!").

What Jonas wasn't surprised to find was the complete and utter lack of patrons in the bar. At the present time, there were only two yokels in the joint. One, gnawing on a toothpick and using a filthy rag to wipe out a glass that he had probably been wiping all night, who Jonas could only assume was the proprietor of this classy establishment, which left the other, wearing a truck driver's cap and nursing a Schlitz with a cigarette between his fingers, to be the racist owner of the poorly parked pick-up truck outside. Both men looked up when Jonas and Mary Beth entered the bar, but neither gave any acknowledgement to their presence. Mary Beth leaned in towards Jonas.

"I'm going to use the loo," She whispered and then bounded off towards the back of bar where a hand-carved wooden sign reading "Pissers and Shitters" hung.

Nothing but class in Harrisburg.

Jonas glanced around the barroom, unable and unwilling to hide his amazement at the bar's ambiance, before he bellied up to the bar itself. The bartender didn't say anything to him. He just kept on wiping his clearly disgusting mug.

At this point, does that even constitute as cleaning? It's more like rearranging filth.

Jonas cleared his throat and nodded at the barkeep. The man, taking his sweet time, set the glass on the counter in front of himself and tossed the filthy dishrag sideways into a pickle-bucket filled with murky, gray water.

54

"Whaddaya want?" The bartender asked, not moving from where he was planted behind the bar. Jonas realized quickly that he probably wouldn't get any answers if he didn't order a drink. He was fairly certain he wouldn't get any answers even if he did order a drink, but his odds seemed slightly better. He groped into his pocket and laid a crumpled five-dollar bill on the counter.

"Gimme what he's having," He said, tilting his head towards the trucker. The bartender reached into the cooler, pulled out a beer, and popped the top. He strode across the floor, slammed the beer can down, and snatched the fiver up.

"Thanks," Jonas said, bringing the lukewarm can to his lips and taking a swallow of foam. He set the beer can back down before him, "Hey, either of you know how to get back to Westfield from here?"

The bartender paused momentarily but didn't respond. He glanced at the truck driver before he continued walking to the tin cash box on the bar back. Jonas brought the can up to his lips again.

Well, this was a waste of my fucking time.

And my five spot.

"The fuck you goin' to Westfield fer?"

Jonas stopped with the beer can halfway back down to the bar. He turned towards the truck driver, who was staring straight ahead, arms crossed on the bar, snuffing out the remnants of his cigarette in the dirty ashtray at his elbow. Jonas wasn't sure why, but he felt goosebumps form on his forearm.

They breed all kinds of crazy up here.

55

He swallowed the piss beer in his mouth and cleared his throat, knowing full well that it would be best to keep the conversation to a bare minimum.

"I just need to gas up," Jonas said. The trucker wheeled in his seat and sprang to his feet facing Jonas with such ferocity that Jonas sprang backwards in his chair, certain that his heartbeat could be heard on the NASA space station.

"Harrisburg gas don't do it fer ya'?" The trucker spat through aged yellow teeth. Jonas snapped his eyes away from the man's rotting mouth and locked eyes with the truck driver. Unease poured over him as though someone had just dropped a bucket of ice water over his head. The man's eyes were worse than his teeth. Wild eyes, the color of burnt charcoal set upon bloodshot red and jaundice yellow. The hazy pupil in his left eye was permanently dilated. Jonas realized that he was staring, with "The Tell-Tale Heart" playing in the forefront of his mind. He dropped his eyes from the man's eyes to his chest. Sewn onto the upper right breast of his faded and ratty work shirt was the name "Lyle".

That's kind of like an introduction. Pleased to meetcha, Lyle.

"No. Not at all," Jonas grunted, regaining some semblance of his composure and shaking his head. He allowed his breath a moment to catch up with him, "I would be more than pleased to support the local economy of Harrisburg if the gas stations were open. But I gotta fill up because I'm almost on empty and I have many miles to travel before I sleep…"

You're rambling. Stop rambling.

Lyle took three lurching steps towards Jonas, his hand holding the bar to keep him steady as his beaten work boots slapped the floor. He snorted as he drew in a breath.

"Didja know that the bastards in Westfield are nothing but heathens?" Lyle growled. He was almost on top of Jonas now and Jonas could smell the reeking mix of working man's sweat coupled with stale yeast and barely rolling of the man's body. He could feel the man's wild eyes searing into him.

Jonas' words almost got lost coming through his throat, but he managed to eek out a stammered, "Excuse me?"

Jesus. This guy is drunker than a skunk and batshit crazy to boot. I don't give a shit if I have to wander Wisconsin's asshole for the tail end of the remainder of my life. I gotta get out of here.

Jonas had never turned down a bar fight yet. Most of the bar fights Jonas had been in u p to this point had been for a particular reason. An alkie hitting on his girlfriend, a douchebag frat-boy shooting his mouth off, some jagoff looking for a fight and coming to the wrong place at the wrong time. But he had never been in a fight with an overbearing, homegrown maniac and the half-with bearing down on him seemed like he was crazy enough to kill a stranger as much as look at him. Couple that insanity with the completely disinterested bartender, who had returned to gnawing his toothpick and cleaning his glass, and Jonas was a split-second from bolting through the door. His old man had always told him never to back down from a fight but running home with your tail tucked between your legs didn't sound so bad when the alternative was losing your tail altogether and being buried in a shallow grave.

Then he remembered Mary Beth was in the bathroom.

Oh, come on. What the fuck is she doing in there?

Jonas decided it didn't matter. He didn't want to know and, regardless of how irritating Mary Beth was, there was absolutely no way he could tuck and run without Mary Beth in tow. He didn't even want to think of the consequences to that action. It would be a toss-up, but he was pretty sure that Mindy would be harder on him than Lyle ever could be.

As if on cue, Lyle's face was inches from his own. Lyle slammed his palm down on the bar. It made a sound like a shotgun blast. Jonas winced.

I hope the bartender is willing and able to read me my last rites.

"Mother fucking heathens," Lyle hissed, "God damned, dirty heathen sons of bitches. The whole lot of 'em."

"I'm… I'm not sure I'm following," Jonas stuttered, trying his hardest to keep the crazy guy from snapping entirely while simultaneously trying to keep the man's spittle from hitting him. Lyle turned towards Jonas, yanking back the sleeve of his work shirt. Jonas met his gaze, wide eyed, for the second time in as many minutes, solely because he wasn't quite sure where else to look.

"Lookit this," Lyle shouted, as though he was reading Jonas' scattered thoughts, "Lookit what those heathens did to me."

Jonas tore his eyes away from the reddening face and looked down at the outstretched forearm that was being thrust out before him. Jagged scar tissue crisscrossed the length of inflamed pink burn marks that crawled over every inch of the man's arm.

It's like looking at a topographic map. Are those the Andes?

Jonas turned away from the arm, back to his warm beer on the counter. He reached out and brought the can to his lips, chugging half of it down. His entire body was covered with perspiration, over ever inch of his skin. He slammed the beer back to the counter and drew in a deep breath. Lyle leaned in even closer, speaking in a low, gruff whisper directly into Jonas ear.

"The rest of me looks the same way under these clothes," He whispered, his words grating like sandpaper against Jonas' cardrum.

Is this a pick-up line?

Come the fuck on, Mary Beth, hurry the fuck up.

"Those heathens in Westfield," Lyle continued, "They're ravenous. They have a church all to theyselves."

What the fuck does that even mean?

Move your ass, Mary Beth.

"They done come for me when I was just a boy," Lyle said, tugging down the sleeve of his work shirt and stumbling slowly back across the floor to his barstool. He sank back down in his seat, "They done come for me in the middle of the night. We was camping when they done come for me. Come for me. Gagged me, so mama and my daddy couldn't hear 'em draggin'

59

me away. They come and got me to use as they sac-roe-fishul lamb."

Sweet, merciful mother of God, what the hell kind of place did I walk into?

Is Mary Beth still alive in there?

Lyle picked up his Schlitz and took a long pull. Jonas started to follow suit, thinking that all of the craziness had come to an end. The beer was halfway to his mouth when Lyle started talking again. Jonas almost dropped the beer.

Oh, for the love of.... Come on, Mary Beth! Let's go!

"The sheriff found me before they was through," Lyle said, "They had me laid out on a burning stack a wood. They had covered me with kerosene and was cutting into me, mumblin' and chantin' away in some sorta devil language. Sounded like they was speakin' in tongues. They said it was to make they crops grow faster. Better. But I knows they just had all they screws a little too loose."

There seems to be a lot of screws loose around this place. Somebody needs to get their ass up here with a toolbox.

"I know it's been a long, long while, but they is still out there, those Westfield heathens," Lyle muttered, "And mark my goddamn words. I'll have my revenge before I go. I swear to it. Somebody up there is gonna pay."

Lyle took another long pull from his bottle and lowered his head to pull out his cigarettes just as Mary Beth was coming out of the bathroom.

Jesus. If that isn't the most beautiful goddamned sight I've ever seen.

Jonas stood quickly from his chair, almost knocking it over behind him as he subtly but furiously motioned Mary Beth towards the door. Mary Beth was messing with her purse and was completely oblivious to the horror on Jonas' face and the terror in his eyes.

"Did you get directions?"

"I got enough," Jonas hissed.

"So, you know how to get back to the campground?" Mary Beth asked. Lyle raised his head and looked at Mary Beth. His charcoal gray eyes seemed to grow two shades darker.

"You's campin' in Westfield?"

Jonas felt his heart drop and his stomach bounce to catch it. He shook his head violently, but his words got caught in his throat. Before he could untangle his vocal cords to speak, Mary Beth nodded.

"Yep," She said, "We're on a weekend retreat with some friends."

"Where ya' camping at?"

Jonas started walking towards the door, hoping Mary Beth would take the hint and follow. Unfortunately, she didn't.

"We're camping on a piece of land just off of…" She started, but paused, trying to recollect the name of the street that Mindy's land was on.

Thank God for her stupidity.

61

Jonas strode briskly back across the barroom and grabbed hold of Mary Beth's arm, just above the elbow. Mary Beth turned to shoot an icy glare at him with a look of utter shock emblazoned on her face.

"Ouch, Jonas," She cried, "That really hurts." Jonas nodded and raised his eyebrows, his eyes darting towards the front door.

"We have to get a move on," He stated bluntly, rapidly moving his eyes towards the exit, "Ryan and Whit are probably wondering what the hell happened to us in here."

"Oh, right," She said, turning towards the exit. Jonas released her arm.

Finally, we can get out of here before she went and...

Mary Beth stopped short, turning back to Lyle, a look of enlightenment falling across her face. Jonas' mouth formed into an "O" of terror as he lunged forward with his hand out in an attempt to cover Mary Beth's mouth. He was too late.

"Bear Paw Road!" She stated, "We're camping off Bear Paw Road."

Jonas' hand fell limply to his side. The bar succumbed to silence. Jonas looked from Mary Beth's overly happy, stupid, smiling face to Lyle's dark profile. Lyle slowly placed a cigarette between his lips and flicked his lighter. The soft orange glow illuminated his ruddy complexion as he took a long, deep drag off of his cigarette. The lighter puffed out and Lyle turned slowly in his chair to lock eyes with Jonas. A second wave of flop sweat erupted from every pore on Jonas' body as Lyle's mouth slowly turned up at the corners. He took another drag off of his cigarette and removed it from his lips, giving Jonas a devilish smile and exposing his discolored teeth. He accompanied the smile with a little wave.

"Maybe we'll catch up with y'all soon."

Jonas turned on his heels and stormed directly out the front door.

Fuck consequences. If she doesn't move, she stays.

The Ride Back

"What took you so long?"

"Did you guys get directions?"

Mary Beth barely had time to close her door, let alone answer Whitney and Ryan's questions before Jonas threw the car in reverse and slammed on the gas. He cranked the wheel, put the car in drive, and slammed the gas again, the car tire's screeching as they bit into the road. Ryan grabbed the back of the driver's seat to steady himself.

"Wow. Grampy's driving like Vin Diesel," He quipped, "I didn't realize NASCAR had a senior division."

Ryan waited for a scathing comeback but Jonas didn't respond. He had barely even registered Ryan's comment. Though he kept his eyes on the road, his thoughts were playing and replaying the scene that had just taken place at Herod's Hillbilly House of Hell. Whitney glanced over her shoulder at Ryan and he shrugged his shoulders. They all drove on in silence for several minutes, until they reached the edge of Harrisburg.

"They seemed nice," Mary Beth stated, staring out the window at the darkened landscape, "Too bad Whit isn't old enough to drink yet. We could've hung out there for a bit."

You have got to be fucking kidding me.

"Nice?" Jonas snarled, taking his eyes off the road to shoot Mary Beth a death glare through the rearview mirror, "They seemed nice?" Mary Beth jerked her head forward at the sound of

64

Jonas' voice. Jonas turned his head to glare at her with even more fury.

Oh man… Give it to her.

"They seemed like fucking lunatics," Jonas spat at her before returning his eyes to the road, "And do you know why they seemed like lunatics? Because that's exactly what they fucking were!"

"I didn't get that vibe from them at all," Mary Beth said, bringing her hand up to her chest in surprise.

"You didn't get that vibe because you were barely fucking there!" Jonas laughed, "You were shitting your brains out for half an hour while I was being accosted by those crazy fucking lunatics." Mary Beth gasped and her jaw just about hit the floormat. She looked at Ryan, then back at Jonas, then back at Ryan, her mouth moving frantically but no words came out.

"Whoa," Ryan breathed, "What the fuck happened back there?"

"Mary Beth's best friend forever, Lyle the fucking lunatic, went damn near apeshit on me while she was taking her sweet time in the toilet," Jonas snapped. Mary Beth gasped a second time and her voice squeaked as she tried to think of something to say to rebuke Jonas' claims. Jonas held up a hand to silence her. Mary Beth's mouth closed with a sickening, wet plop. Whether it was because she could actually feel the anger emanating from Jonas' entire body or because she decided that she didn't have a leg to stand on, didn't really matter to Jonas. She shut her trap all

65

the same and Jonas launched into a recap of what had happened in the bar.

"You told them where we were camping?" Whitney asked when Jonas had finished his story, wheeling around in her seat to face Mary Beth. Mary Beth shrugged it off.

"The guy seemed harmless to me," She defended herself, "And, anyway, I didn't tell him exactly where we were staying. All I said was 'off Bear Paw Road'."

"That's so much better," Ryan scoffed, "Because a local guy from around these parts would have such a hard time figuring out where Bear Paw Road is." Mary Beth shook her head and grunted before returning to staring out the window. A small part of Jonas felt somewhat vindicated.

At least they're on my side.

"You all know that this is how horror movies start, right?" Whitney asked in a poor attempt to lighten the mood. The question hung in the air with a misty smell until Ryan finally gave up a half-assed pity laugh that sounded slightly more like a cough than a chuckle.

"If that's the case… Who goes first?" Ryan asked. Whitney brought her finger up to her chin and sat in silence for a moment, pondering the question.

"Well, it can't be Jonas. He's the driver," She responded, "And it can't be me because I'm the innocent one. It must be you, Ryan."

"Dammit, how did I wind up as the token black guy?"

66

Ryan and Whitney commenced into a storm of giggles. Jonas clenched his teeth and stared at the road before him, not finding a single, solitary lick of humor in the whole situation.

I just had a run in with the extended members of a crossbreeding experiment between the Addams' family and the Manson family. I didn't even want to come camping in the first place and now, instead of camping, we're lost beyond any sort of recognition. We may as well be on the surface of the moon. Laugh it up, chuckleheads, because there's a good chance that we're never getting back home in one piece. It's only a matter of fucking time before we wind up back in Harrisburg, where Lyle and his cousins are gonna make us squeal like piggies until...

Jonas slammed on his brakes so hard that the other passengers in the car cried out in unison. Ryan pitched forward, hitting his face on the back of the driver's seat and knocking off his glasses. Both he and Whitney stopped their giggling. Mary Beth pulled in a deep breath of air.

"What the fuck are you doing, man?" Ryan asked angrily, rubbing his cheek with one hand while he reached down to find his glasses with the other. Jonas didn't answer. He threw the car in reverse and looked over his shoulder out the back window. After a few feet, he put the car back into drive and turned off the pavement and onto a barely noticeable dirt sideroad.

"This is how we get back to camp," He said. Whitney looked out the window.

"I definitely remember this."

Back at Camp

The tree covered tunnel of a road back to camp was even longer and twice as creepy as Jonas had remembered from the initial journey a mere handful of hours before. The surrounding trees and brush threw nondescript shadows as the car's headlights washed over the, and the road itself, with every rut and bounce, seemed to go on forever. Jonas let his eyes dart from side to side, surveying the darkened wilderness.

Lyle and his pals are going to pop out from behind one of these trees at any second and take this car by storm. They're going to overthrow the driver and pull their victims from the interior. God willing, they'll kill us immediately because, if they don't, I can damn near guarantee that we're in for a world of hurt.

Jonas realized that he was holding his breath. He let it out in a single whoosh that was silenced by the noise of rocks and dirt hitting the underside of the car. As they passed the camper, Jonas felt his breath hitch again, his heart slapping against the inside of his ribcage like a tom-tom drum on methamphetamines. But no one leapt from the dense thicket of trees to overpower them. No one sprang from the darkness. Nothing happened. So, Jonas kept driving and, soon enough, the car emerged from the tunnel of trees, unscathed, and they entered into the clearing.

"We've been gone for exactly one hour," Whitney pointed out, sounding like a very precocious six year old who was learning to tell time. Jonas put the car in park and gave a slight nod, not even pretending to care how long they had been gone.

The important thing is that we're back at camp and we're not dead.

Not yet.

"Thankfully, the worst is behind us," Ryan stated as he exited the vehicle. Whitney and Mary Beth quickly followed suit. Jonas, however, remained in the car behind the steering wheel, trying in vain to push away the feeling of dread that had settled into his stomach like a cannonball. When he finally calmed down enough to function like a normal human being, he eased the car door open and stepped out onto the spongy, dew covered grass. He walked across the moonlit clearing, back towards his fellow campers.

"Did you get lost?" Mindy asked. Jonas shook his head.

"Nope."

"Liar," Mindy said as a smile flowed across her lips, "You followed the curve, didn't you?" Jonas nodded, sheepishly.

"We ended up in Harrisburg," Whitney explained.

"Twice," Ryan interrupted.

And then Mary Beth opened her big, fat fucking mouth and drew some lunatic with a personal vendetta a treasure map to exactly where we've set up camp. Now we're going to be brutally attacked in the middle of the night by either a wandering group of complete nut jobs from Harrisburg or a cult of heathens from Westfield. Kind of like the Jets and the Sharks, only with less choreography and more violence.

All in all, I'd say it was a pretty good trip.

"Did you guys get gas?" Cal asked from the firepit. The flames stood in his eyes, dancing in his pupils like merry little demons. Chris set his beer down and leaned forward in his chair.

"Please tell me you got gas," he pleaded, "This kid has a hard-on for the quads. He's been talking about them non-stop since you left."

Jonas closed his eyes and shook his head slowly, "Sorry, man. We never actually made it to a gas station."

"Dammit," Cal grunted, tossing his poking stick into the fire with ferocity. Jonas raised his eyebrows.

"Easy, killer," Ryan said, "We'll get gas tomorrow. We've got three whole days to hang out up here."

Cal nodded but he didn't even try to hide the pouty look on his face. Jonas kicked a clod of dirt with his foot.

"I'm sorry, guys. I fucked up. I had no idea where the hell we were."

All I knew for sure is that I wanted to get out of wherever the fuck it was as fast as humanly possible.

Garrett, who was sitting on a chair beside Chris, leaned forward, "Don' worry 'boutit, man. Chris n'me been up hea' a hund'd times and we still get los'." Jonas nodded. He knew Garrett was trying to help but he didn't particularly care what he had to say.

If I can't find m way around her better than these almost backwoods morons, that's not saying very much for me. Plus, not only did I get lost, but I look like the mother of all assholes to

70

*these fuckers. They're probably all thinking, "Doug wouldn't
have gotten lost."*

Well, fuck them.

And fuck him.

"We ended up in Harrisburg the last time we were up here,"
Chris recalled, slurring his words slightly, "Blew right through
that shithole town as fast as the wheels would carry us. Creepy
as all hell."

"It didn't seem all that bad," Mary Beth said, "It reminded me
of Detroit."

Jesus, Mary, and Joseph... That's it. That's all I can stand.

*If she says that Harrisburg reminded her of Detroit one more
time, I'm going to blow.*

Jonas threw a glare at Mary Beth and turned away from the
circle.

"I gotta go to the bathroom."

Outhouse

Jonas had not yet been blessed to use the outdoor plumbing at the Westfield Hilton and he was terribly put off at the idea of his trip to the outhouse. Aside from the fact that he was certain that it was crawling with any number of furry, human sized insects and it most likely smelled the way he imagined a week old, neglected corpse would smell, it was actually the view that was the most off putting. The outhouse, in order to ensure maximum privacy and minimum stench, faced away from the campground proper and looked out into the woods. The pitch-black darkness of the desolate woods to be more precise.

Where the children of Westfield's God are hiding.

Waiting.

Watching.

Jonas fished around in his pocket for his flashlight as his thoughts returned to Lyle of Harrisburg and the ominous words he had spoken. He shook his head, trying to clear his mind of the hillbilly prophet, and a chill coursed through his entire body.

"Fucking hick," He mumbled as he continued to pat his pockets.

"What fucking hick?"

Jonas' head snapped up and he leaped backwards, away from the voice that came at him from the darkness. Instinctively, his hand went to his back pocket where he kept his switchblade. He remembered, as his hand touched the back of his jeans, that he had left in his duffle bag back in his tent. Right next to his flashlight. His hand curled into a fist and he brought it back up to his chest. If he was going to die, he was going to go down swinging.

Before Jonas could unfreeze and throw a punch, a silhouette of the body the voice belonged to came into view. It was just Coral. Jonas let out a sigh of relief.

"When did you get here?" Jonas asked, hearing his voice crack as he tried to play it cool. His nerves downshifted and his heartbeat started to return to normal. Coral cocked an eyebrow at him as she fully emerged from the shadow of the outhouse and walked past him on her way back to the firepit.

"Kevin and I got here about forty-five minutes ago," She said, not turning back to look at him, "You were in town getting gas."

Mindy had mentioned something about Coral being late to arrive. That was why they set up her tent. Coral had to work and didn't want to set her tent up in the dark. Well, it was definitely dark now. Jonas offered up a small wave as Coral walked away, realizing almost immediately that she couldn't see him in the inky blackness. Not that it would've mattered even if she could. Jonas always got the feeling that Coral didn't care for him much. It never really bothered him. He had enough on his plate.

Especially now that you know there are psychos in the woods. Psychos looking for sacrifices.

There are no psychos. There are no heathens. There is nothing to worry about.

Jonas stumble stepped through the darkness, using his hand on the roughhewn wood of the outhouse's exterior to guide him, to

73

the door. He pulled his lighter from his pocket, flicked it, and, using the dim orange glow, peered inside. After a glance around and a momentary second thought, he stepped inside. He gave the interior a closer inspection, scanning the walls, the seat, and the roll of toilet paper itself.

There's nothing to worry about except monstrous spiders.

He gave a full body shudder at the thought and began carefully weighing his options. After concluding that, over the course of three days he would inevitably have to deal with the outhouse sooner or later, he began to unbuckle his belt. He turned to cast a glance over his shoulder, through the open doorway behind him, at the foreboding void of the forest.

If you gaze long enough into the abyss, the abyss will gaze back.

You can feel it, can't you?

Feel what?

The eyes. The eyes on you. They're watching you.

Shut the fuck up.

They're watching. They're waiting.

Jonas paused, his pants still buttoned, eyes fixed on the darkness. He didn't want to let Lyle, that crazy redneck, get inside his head. But his subconscious wasn't being entirely ridiculous, was it? Something seemed... off. There was a slight feeling of being watched. The uncomfortable feeling of someone's gaze trying to engulf him. It was making it hard to breathe. He tried to push the feeling away, tried to convince himself that he was just being foolish, but the hairs on the nape of his neck refused to lay flat. He shook his head and bucked his belt back up. He would try again later, maybe when it was daylight. He stepped out of the outhouse and stared straight ahead into the forest. He took a step forward. Then another, squinting his eyes.

What's that?

What's what?

That… Right there… is that a shadow? Is it…

"What the fuck are you staring at?"

Jonas wheeled around, throwing himself off balance and not quite able to stop the eek that escaped his throat. A strong hand grabbed his upper arm as he stumbled backwards. Chris, holding a beer and swaying ever so slightly, helped him regain his balance. He was looking at Jonas quizzically with one eyebrow raised.

"There was… I thought…" Jonas stammered, trying to explain, turning towards the woods to point out the shadow he had seen, but it was already gone. Jonas scanned the forest quickly, trying to spot it again, but to no avail. Chris raised his other eyebrow, waiting for Jonas to finish his sentence. Jonas swallowed the growing lump in his throat and shook his head, "Nothing. I just thought I saw something in the woods."

Did you really not see anything?

"Where's your flashlight, man?" Chris asked. Jonas shook his head again and shrugged, feeling like a stupid child who was being scolded for making a stupid mistake.

Doug would've remembered his flashlight.

75

Shut up.

Doug wouldn't have been terrified of the absolute nothing that you just saw.

Seriously, shut up.

Chris shook his head and laughed, "Man, you should always bring your flashlight everywhere out here, especially to the can. It's dark and you don't really know your way around."

I'll give you one guess who always knew his way around.

I swear to God... Shut up.

"Now," Chris said, followed by a commercial interruption sponsored by a loud belch, "If you'll excuse me, I have to take a piss pretty bad." He started forward, stumbling off and heading deeper into the woods. Jonas watched him leave.

"The outhouse is over here," Jonas called out. Chris laughed again.

"I'm not using that thing," He said, "It's fucking gross. Fulla spiders."

"Where's your flashlight?"

"I don't need one," he replied with yet another laugh, "I know my way around. Doug and me have been all over these woods."

Of course you have.

Jonas nodded and the slumped back through the dark towards the firepit. As he drew closer, he saw that only two campers remained in the chairs surrounding the pit. Narissa and Mindy. Jonas stood behind Mindy's chair, leaning over to kiss her on top of her head.

"Where'd everybody go?"

Mindy craned her neck to look up at Jonas and he could see from the way her eyelids were drooping that she had been dozing off as he came up. She shook the sleepiness from her head and stifled a yawn.

"They went to bed," She informed him in the Lauren Bacall voice that she always got when she first woke up, "I was waiting up for you to get back so we could hit the hay."

"That's the best idea I've heard all night," Jonas said, bending down to plant another kiss on her forehead, "Let's hit that hay." Mindy smiled and slowly got to her feet. She took two steps towards the tent and then stopped, putting her hand to her head, before turning around.

"Oh, Narissa," She said, remembering that her friend was sitting across from her. She walked back towards her seat, "I forgot Chris left."

"Don't sit up on account of me. Chris'll be back in just a few," Narissa said, standing from her own chair and stretching her back, "I'm gonna turn in, too. Chris is a big boy. He'll find his way to bed."

"You sure you aren't putting just a little too much faith in him?" Mindy laughed.

"Sometimes, I think I am," Narissa retorted. She turned towards her tent with a wave to say good night.

"To sleep it is," Mindy stated, resting her head on Jonas' shoulder and kissing his neck, "I'm exhausted."

"Yeah," Jonas agreed, "I legit feel like I could sleep for days." They made their way to their tent by the fading orange glow of the dying campfire. Mindy unzipped the door and crawled inside. Jonas, taking a moment to watch her from behind, started to climb in after her. He paused for a moment and then reached for his bag. He unzipped it and began rustling around in the outer pocket.

"What are you doing?" Mindy asked as she unclasped her bra. Jonas rubbed his tongue along his front teeth.

"I gotta brush," He told her. Mindy rolled her eyes and Jonas went on mock defensive, "What? My teeth feel like their covered in moss."

"All right," Mindy replied with a yawn, "I'll be right here. But I can't promise I'll be awake when you get back."

"I'll only be gone a minute."

If the ghouls don't getcha first.

No Rest for the Weary

"What the fuck was that?" Jonas asked, bolting upright on the air mattress. Mindy didn't even bother to move.

"It's the wind, Jonas," She mumbled, "The wind or some sort of animal." Jonas lay his head back down on the pillow and draped an arm over Mindy.

Just the wind.

It's never just the wind.

"Non-campers," Mindy muttered and moved closer to him, turning her head slightly to kiss his neck. Jonas didn't respond. He was too focused on the sounds of desolation coming from outside the thin polyester walls of the tent. Even though he was a "non-camper", tried and true, he had to admit that it was pretty serene out here. Aside from the wind or the animals, whatever it was that had jostled him from his sleep, there wasn't a single sound out there. There was no drunken catcalling from the bars, no sound of tires screeching on pavement or motors revving on the streets, no early morning garbage trucks or delivery vans. He closed his heavy eyelids, took in the silence that surrounded him, and felt comfort in the warmth of Mindy's body next to him.

Mindy.

If asked to pinpoint what, exactly, it was about Mindy, Jonas didn't think he could. The two of them seemed like a conundrum. She was, after all the queen of the rednecks, outdoorsy to a fault, loved country music, and could boot, scoot, and boogie with the best of them. Jonas, however, couldn't. He was a city kid or, at the very least, a suburbia kid and, either way you cut it, he was and had never been the king of anything. He had never once had an inkling to pack a pair or two of underwear and head out into the nearest woods to live off the land. The closest he ever got to country music was listening to one of two Johnny Cash albums he owned, Live at Folsom and Greatest Hits.

But, as the saying goes, you can't choose the ones you love. When Jonas had met Mindy something had sparked between them and there had been immediate fireworks. She was his opposite but, again, as they say, opposites attract. They had started seeing each other, very slowly, and, eventually, one thing lead to another, which lead to another, which lead to a great deal of alcohol, which lead them to exactly where they were right now.

Which, let's face it, isn't the best place to be.

In a tent in the middle of nowhere?

Well, that… but also in this rocky stage we're in.

You just need to get your shit together. Then everything will be smooth sailing again.

Easier said than done.

You could start by writing that book.

If I had my laptop and if no one else was around, I could seriously get some major league words on the page.

And writing was exactly what he needed to get done. Writing had always been something of an escape for Jonas but, recently, it had become so much more. At the same time, however, it had also become so much less. He had started sending off some query letters for his work to publishing houses and, as of a month ago, he had finally been approached to have one of his stories put between covers. While this was fantastic news from all angles, the potential success had exactly the opposite effect for Jonas' creativity. Almost immediately upon receiving the e-mail, Jonas had suffered a crippling case of writer's block, the author's cancer, and he hadn't been able to get anything of note, let alone anything at all, down on paper for the past several weeks. He had to come up with something that would sell but, as of right now, he had no idea what that something was and his deadline was approaching fast.

His first novel, a noir piece about a gun for hire, was supposed to be his way to break onto the scene. It had taken him forever to write and he had been pouring every last bit of his blood, sweat, and tears into it for years. The publisher, a small imprint that specialized in hard-boiled pulp pieces, had ate it up and had offered to put it out. The problem was that it was presently being bounced around in the endless hell that was the publishing industry.

Just thinking about the whole ordeal was enough to make Jonas' skin break out in a cold, clammy sweat. He had always told himself that he would never be a "sell out" author, writing for the sole purpose of collecting a paycheck. He had always said that he wanted nothing more than to make a living writing. Once he got his first book published, all he wanted to do was to be able to make a little bit of money so he could pay his bills. He didn't even want to quit his job at the bookstore. He loved his job. He wanted writing to be what got him by. That was it. Just to get by. So long as the bills got paid and he was able to put food on his table, everything was kosher. He didn't necessarily need the shiny car, the fancy watch, all of the other expensive shit that went along with it. Granted, he wouldn't turn it away if it happened, but he didn't care about that.

Unfortunately, the bills just refused to wait until his book was published. They just kept piling up, leaving Jonas with the small amount of cash he had growing smaller with every passing day, thereby keeping his already overworked mind constantly at unease. It had started out as a problem he was facing all by himself but, over the past few months, it had started to take its toll on his relationship with Mindy. If it had just been him, it wouldn't have been a big deal if he couldn't buy anything but ramen noodles and cigarettes. But now he couldn't afford to buy Mindy anything. He couldn't afford to take her out on dates. Hell, he could barely afford to put gas in his car so he could go sit on her couch.

Granted, Mindy assured him, on a regular basis, that she didn't need those things. He just couldn't wrap his head around it. He needed to do those things for her. He wanted to do those things for her. He wanted to buy her house, with a yard, where they could spend their days, start a family, three kids and a dog, and live that fairy tale romance. But he was finding it harder and harder to see those dreams coming to fruition with the mountain of bills that loomed over his head and out onto every single horizon before him. No matter where he looked, he couldn't see anything but bill after bill after bill. Mindy could swear up and down that she didn't mind being poor as long as she had Jonas. Jonas couldn't believe that.

Even Doug was making decent cash... and he cleaned bathrooms for a living.

What if this is what my life is going to be like forever?

Before his mind had a chance to answer, sleep overtook the shell of a man.

Morning Has Broken

Jonas was awakened for the second time by what sounded like bats fluttering nervously about his eardrums. He was awake, but he kept his eyes sealed shut, furrowing his brow as he listened to the endless flapping bouncing around in his head.

I don't want to see the look on the damned things face before it bites me on the neck.

He became quickly aware that the inside of the tent felt like the interior of an oven. Jonas could guess by the amount of heat that the tent had managed to suck up like a sponge that the night had somehow managed to slip away when he had closed his eyes.

Mindy's voice, breathy and sultry, commandeered Jonas' hearing, drowning out the bat's wings ever so slightly, "You can't knock on a tent like you knock on a door."

That's a good one. I should use that.

Jonas pried his eyes open, feeling the irritation spread through his entire body. He sat up, wiping his grimy, sweaty face and looked bleary eyed at his watch. He couldn't make out the numbers through his sleep deprived eyes but he knew that it was half-past too fucking early.

"You need to get up," Ryan's voice came from outside the tent, "Like, right now. We have a fucking problem."

"What time is it?" Jonas asked, stifling a yawn. Mindy shook her head in disgust.

"Too early for whatever shit is going on," She grumbled. She threw back the sleeping bag and got to her knees, reaching for her pants. Jonas raised his eyes as he watched her stretch to grab them. Her ass looked dynamite. He was tempted to try to pull her back to the floor of the tent but, when she tugged her pants on and sat down to yank on her shoes, he saw the scowl on her face. Timing was everything and this was definitely not the right time. She unzipped the tent and angrily made her way outside.

"Leave it open," Jonas said, "I'm coming too." He pulled his pants on and put his bare feet into his boots before stepping out after Mindy.

Maybe Mary Beth got eaten by a bear.

A smiled crossed his face as his imagination was imbedded with the image of a huge grizzly bear standing in the middle of the clearing, cheeks bulging out, chewing the remainder of Mary Beth's leg that still protruded from its mouth. Jonas bit the insides of his cheeks to keep from laughing out loud.

There is seriously something wrong with me.

"What the fuck is going on?" Mindy's angry voice snapped him back to reality in a jiffy. She was standing just a few feet away, staring at Whitney and Ryan, who were huddled together. From the corner of his eye, Jonas saw Garrett, standing far too close, with his arms crossed, a cigarette dangling from his lips. The power of suggestion made Jonas pat his pockets, looking for his own smokes.

Shit. Must've left them in the tent.

Garrett held out the pack and his lighter, offering a smoke to Jonas in a gesture of cigarette smoker unity. Jonas nodded his gratitude and snaked a cigarette from the pack. As he lit his cigarette, his eyes went back to Mindy. She was standing across the clearing, one hand against her forehead, the other was outstretched at her side, swinging wildly about. Jonas had no idea what she was gesturing at but she didn't look happy. His eyes followed her arm to the empty patch of grass beside where they had all parked their cars. He saw nothing out of the norm, aside from a few tire marks that had matted down the grass where they had driven in across the field. He took in a breath to ask what was happening. Then he noticed the tires. His words caught in his throat.

Every single tire on every single car was flat.

Welcome to Westfield. Home of the crazy natives. Enjoy your stay.

Plan

Everyone stood in stunned silence, staring at the tires as though, with enough eye contact, they would magically inflate. Mindy shook her head and pointed at the cars, just in case anyone standing around had not noticed them yet.

"Seriously?" She screamed, "What the fuck happened?"

Ryan shook his head and gave a small shrug, "I don't know, Mindy. I came out here a few minutes ago to get my water from the car and this is what I found." Mindy's face went from red to a shade of purple as she let out a guttural, inhuman bellow of sheer, unadulterated rage.

"What's goin' on?" The five campers who had been staring at the cars turned in an almost perfect unison that Jonas thought probably would've been a pretty fair bit of comedic choreography had the circumstances been different. Coral, Kevin, Mary Beth, Cal, and Narissa were walking across the field from their tents. Each of them wore a look of equal parts preemptive worry mixed with sleepiness plastered on their faces.

"What's with the yelling?" Coral asked with a yawn, "Everything okay?"

"Somebody let all the air out of the tires," Jonas said, running his fingers through his hair. Garrett walked a few paces to get a better look at the cars. He squatted down beside his jeep like a Native American Indian guide and took a deep drag off of his cigarette.

"Th'ain't deflat'd," He mumbled, shaking his head, "They's slashed." He took the cigarette from his lips, holding it between his index and middle fingers, and pointed to a jagged tear in the tire wall.

That means they have sharp objects.

Crazy people shouldn't be allowed to have sharp objects.

They probably shouldn't be allowed to have objects at all.

"Holy shit. Are you serious?" Cal asked, dropping to one knee beside Garrett and moving his head in close to the tire to get a better look. His jaw fell in awe as Garrett stood up and nodded his head.

"Mmm-hm," Garrett grunted, flicking his cigarette to the side, "This'er wadn't jes ha'mless fun."

"No shit," Mindy snarled, turning away from the vehicles.

"Who would do this?" Coral asked, moving in to rub her hand along the tires of her Corsica.

"Some yokels, maybe?" Kevin offered. Jonas realized that he had never actually heard Kevin speak. He wondered why that was. It was an interesting philosophical question that he wanted to dive deeper into.

This isn't the time nor the place.

"No one even knows we're up here," Coral countered, shaking her head, "We're up here earlier than usual."

Ryan and Whitney both looked to Jonas and the three of them looked slowly towards Mary Beth. She was staring dumbfoundedly at the cars before her. No one said anything out loud as they rejoined everyone to stand in silence and stare at the cars. It felt like they stood there for an eternity.

"What are we going to do?" Whitney finally asked. Jonas jumped when the silence was broken so abruptly. Ryan shrugged his shoulders.

"What can we do?" He replied, "Unless someone brought four spare tires along with them, we have to call for help, right?"

"Each car has a spare tire," Mary Beth announced excitedly. Her face brightened as though she had cracked the case. Jonas gritted his teeth at the very sound of her voice. He looked at his watch.

It's not even seven in the morning and she's already grating on my nerves.

You have more than one left?

"So what?" Mindy snapped. Apparently, Jonas' nerves weren't the only ones being grated.

"Uh, Duh," Mary Beth said, raising her eyebrows as though she was shocked no one else was seeing her brilliant idea, "We could put all the spares on one car and go for help."

"Mmm-mm," Garrett shook his head, "Diff'ent makesnmodels. We don' have fur tyrs'll work t'geth'r." Ryan took his arm from around Whitney and walked towards his car.

"Then we call Triple A," He stated as he pulled open the door. He leaned in and plucked his phone from the cupholder. He was already punching in the numbers as he emerged from his vehicle. He put his phone to his ear and stood silent for a second before thumbing his phone and bringing his arm back down to his side.

89

"I don't have service," He told them. The rest of the campers hurriedly moved away from the semi-circle, making their ways to their cars or tents, each one producing a cell phone. One by one they lifted their phones to their ears and, one by one, looks of disappointment crawled over their faces like wounded animals.

Not a single phone had cell service.

"Good idea, Ryan," Whitney said, trying in vain to lighten the mood.

"If anyone else has a better idea, I'd like to hear it," Ryan said, clearly missing Whitney's poor attempt at humor. Mindy raised her hands.

"Calm down," She said and, even though she was aiming her words at Ryan, Jonas knew she was talking to everyone at once. She looked at the car tires one more time, as if to verify that they were, indeed, still slashed. When she saw that they were, she sighed and continued, "We need to figure out what we're going to do and snapping at one another isn't going to help us at all."

"Kevin and I will walk back to town," Coral said. Garrett shook his head.

"S'long wawk," He informed her. She nodded.

"I'm well aware," She stated bluntly, "But we don't really have any other options."

"We can take the four-wheeler to the end of the dirt road," Kevin said, "That'll cut a few miles off."

"If there's enough gas," Mindy said. Jonas turned to look at her, fully expecting to be on the receiving end of a glare that read, *That is to say, if my boyfriend wasn't such a giant fuck-up.*

She wasn't even looking at him, her eyes were fixated on the tires.

You know she's thinking it though.

"Where are you going to leave the quad?" She asked.

"I can go with them," Cal piped up, "When we get to the end of the driveway, I can bring it back." Coral and Kevin exchanged looks.

"I don't wanna babysit you, kid," Kevin said.

"I'm not a baby," Cal retorted, immediately going on the defensive, "I can take care of myself. I do it all the time at home." Kevin and Cal stared each other down for a moment before Coral stepped between them.

"Whatever. That sounds like the best plan we've got," Coral said, "I'm sure we can catch a ride back from town after we get some help."

From one of the heathens?

It's like leading the lambs to a slaughter.

"All right then. Let's get moving," Kevin said, making his way to the four-wheeler, "We don't want to waste any time, it's gonna be a long trek." He threw his leg over the seat and settled in. He revved up the engine as Coral got on behind him. Cal brought up the rear.

"Be careful," Mindy yelled over the engine, "That's not made for three people and, Cal, don't hot rod on the way back." Kevin nodded and Cal held up a hand to show that he understood.

"See you in a little while," Coral called as Kevin kicked the quad into first gear and tore off towards the street. As the three disappeared into the trees and the sound of the engine slowly dissipated, silence once again overtook the group.

"How far is it to town?" Jonas asked.

"Twen'y...Twen'yfi mile," Garret said with a shrug.

"Jesus," Jonas said, "They'll be lucky to make it back before nightfall." He shivered at the thought of having to walk through that copse of trees in the dark. Garrett nodded his agreement. The group started to make their way back towards the chairs. As they approached, Narissa stopped and, with a puzzled look on her face, she glanced around the campground.

"Hey," She said, with a slight tone of surprise in her voice, "Has anyone seen Chris?"

The Truth About Harrisburg

"I haven't seen him since last night," Jonas said. He looked around the campsite as though they had previously missed him.

"Me neither," Mindy added, shaking her head, "Where the hell did he go?"

"I… I don't know," Narissa stammered. Mindy walked the short distance across the campsite and draped her arm around Narissa.

"What time did he get up?" She asked. Narissa shook her head and her eyes started to water.

"I don't even remember him getting up," She choked, the first trace of worry coming in through her voice. The tears began to roll down her cheeks, "I don't… I don't…"

"Did he even come to bed last night?" Jonas asked. He immediately regretted asking the question when Narissa's legs gave way. She fell to the ground, hands covering her face, gasping for air. Mindy dropped to her knees at Narissa's side and pulled her close, simultaneously shooting Jonas a glare.

Like I was supposed to know she'd keel over if I asked if Chris came to bed.

"Don't freak out," Mindy whispered, "I'm sure that there's a logical explanation."

"What if he was up and out here when whoever slashed the tires was here?" Narissa sobbed, pressing her face into Mindy's shoulder.

If it was Lyle, Chris could've taken him. No problem.

If it was the natives, however… He probably was swept away.
Good night and good luck.

"Chris is a big dude," Ryan chimed in, "If he was out here when the tire slasher showed up, he would've scared him off. Or he would've kicked his ass, but we would've heard that."

Narissa sniffled and nodded her head, but her face remained doubtful. Mindy stroked her hair and pulled her closer, "Chris is absolutely fine."

Sure he is… So long as he hasn't been burned alive to appease the Gods.

Stop it.

Mindy helped Narissa back to her feet and led her back to the campfire. She motioned for the others to follow. The company fell in step but Ryan reached out and grabbed Jonas' elbow, motioning discreetly for him to hold back. They stood in awkward silence until the rest of the campers were out of earshot.

"Dude," Ryan whispered, leaning in towards Jonas' ear, "You don't think this has anything to do with that crazy-ass guy from last night, do you?"

"Not a chance," Jonas stated, probably a bit too quickly, "Lyle was over served but I'm certain he's absolutely harmless."

You fuckin' liar.

"What about the flip side to the coin?" Ryan pressed on, "The people who he said attacked him."

"I doubt if that story has any truth to it at all," Jonas said, "Probably just a byproduct of the booze in his system."

Even you don't believe a word you're saying.

94

C'mon.

Jonas wasn't entirely sure whether or not he believed it. He had a strong, nagging feeling that Lyle wasn't quite as tanked as Jonas would've liked to have believed but he didn't necessarily see the point of riling everyone up over a stupid story that was barely on the cusp of being an urban legend.

"It just seems so weird," Ryan went on, "I mean, after M.B. let it slip last night where we were camping and all. It just seems a bit... I don't know... Coincidental, I guess?"

So it's true. Paranoia is contagious.

"I agree that the timing is weird at best," Jonas said, "But let's just keep this shit quiet for the time being. We don't want to freak everyone out unnecessarily. I mean, Narissa is already on the verge of falling completely off her rocker over this."

Jonas nodded his head in the direction of the campfire. Ryan chewed his lip and nodded his head as he watched Narissa continue to sob into Mindy's shoulder.

"Where do you think Chris is?"

Tied to a stake, surrounded by a circus freakshow of crazy religious zealots, about five seconds away from going up in smoke, give or take.

That is, if they haven't already barbecued him up.

"If he didn't go to bed last night, my guess is that he's probably passed out in the woods someplace, leaned up against a tree," Jonas replied, "The guy was already three sheets to the wind when I turned in. He'd been drinking non-stop since we got here."

"Should we go look for him?"

As the bodiless voice cut into the conversation, Jonas jumped damn near out of his skin. He wheeled around, heart racing, to find Whitney standing just behind them. He shook his head as he tried to regain his composure.

"No. I don't think we should," he gasped, "How long have you been standing there?"

"Pretty much from the moment I saw Ryan trying to be all cloak and dagger," She replied and didn't waste a second further before steering the conversation back to the matter at hand, "Why not?"

Jonas hesitated, trying to figure out the best way to answer that question.

Tell her the truth. Get it out in the open. Say that you don't want to be butchered or sacrificed or mutilated or murdered.

"What time is it? Nine? Ten o'clock?" Jonas asked, raising his arm to look at his watch. Ryan was quicker on the draw.

"7:13," he read, extending his watch for Jonas to look at as if he wouldn't believe it. Jonas double checked his own watch against Ryan's.

"Jesus, if this is what the morning looks like, you can keep it," Jonas muttered. He shook his head and cleared his throat, "It's still early, Whit. Apparently, it's really fucking early. If he's passed out, we'll give him some time to wake up and come in of his own accord."

"Why?"

For the love of God… What's with the third degree?

"Personally, if I were passed out in the woods, I'd rather be allowed to stumble in on my own," Jonas explained, "It's far less embarrassing. Besides, if we form a search party now, there is no way in hell we're going to be able to keep this calm. People are going to freak out. I can guarantee that."

Whitney mulled this over for a moment in her head and then she nodded her approval, seeming to buy into Jonas' rationale. Jonas breathed a silent sigh of relief, thankful that the inquisition had finally come to an end.

"Now," Jonas said, motioning towards the campfire, "All we have to do is steer clear of any conversation that could possibly make Narissa fear for Chris' life."

"I think we can manage that," Ryan said with a laugh, "After all, we're not that stupid."

Jonas and Whitney nodded in agreement. They made their way back to the campfire, the three of them still chuckling over the idea that they would be stupid enough to saunter into the circle and immediately start saying something absolutely clueless. Their chuckles were cut short as they approached the fire. Jonas' jaw dropped and he stopped dead in his tracks.

"...I mean, the guy said, verbatim, that he was nearly killed by the people of Westfield," Mary Beth was saying, leaning in towards Narissa and playing it up for her audience. A melodramatic look of fear and shock emblazoned across her face, "And then, as if that weren't enough, he straight up attacked Jonas!" Jonas, Whitney, and Ryan all looked at each other nervously, their eyes wide, as they mentally exchanged a full conversation in the span of their split-second glances.

Is she a fucking idiot?

What the hell is wrong with her?

We need to diffuse this situation immediately.

"Mary Beth," Jonas said abruptly, cutting her off as she was about to launch further into her story. She seemed pleased to see Jonas and she motioned dramatically for him to take the floor.

"You're here now," She bellowed, "You can tell them firsthand what that lunatic said last night."

"Can you hand me a water?" Jonas said sharply, completely ignoring her comment and not even attempting to be subtle about it. Mary Beth opened the cooler beside her and took out a water. She handed it to Jonas.

"I was trying to explain what happened last night to these guys," She continued, not even skipping a beat and completely oblivious to her surroundings, "Tell then what that looney Lyle said."

"He was drunk. He popped off at the mouth. It happens when people drink," Jonas snapped, not hiding the irritation in his voice. He looked directly at Mary Beth and narrowed his eyes, "And sometimes when they're stone cold sober." Mary Beth's mouth hung agape and she looked momentarily like she had been slapped.

"But... I was just saying..." She stammered, her wet, cow eyes flitting around the circle wildly. Everyone else averted their own eyes.

"Well, don't just say," Jonas commanded, "You weren't even there when he was talking to me. Talking, not attacking. You were in the bathroom the entire time."

Mary Beth's mouth snapped shut with an audible snapping sound. Jonas looked away from her and into the fire. He felt it before he looked up. All eyes were upon him, waiting for some sort of epilogue to conclude the psychotic rant that Mary Beth had been on. He took a long drink from the water bottle.

I pray that everyone here develops an acute case of amnesia and they've all forgotten what we had been talking about before…

"What in the actual fuck is she talking about?" Mindy snapped.

Well, dammit all to hell.

I like Mary Beth a lot better when she's not around.

Jonas brought the bottle away from his lips and cleared his throat before looking up. Just as he had anticipated, all eyes were on him. Mindy's were smoldering. Jonas nodded his head, trying to look nonchalant.

"There was a guy at the bar up the road," He said hesitantly.

Are we doing this? Are we going to try to pin this all on Lyle?

He was crazy.

But was he this crazy?

I don't know! Are there any other options?

It was either him or the cult of Westfield.

You're losing it, man.

"When were you at a bar?" Mindy asked angrily.

99

"Last night," Jonas said, "When we got lost. It was the only place open and I ran in for directions."

"Where at?"

"Harrisburg," Jonas answered, "And yes, there was this guy, Lyle, sitting at the bar. He seemed a little off

A little?

When I asked or directions to Westfield, he kind of got up in my face spouting some complete bullshit

Are you sure it was bullshit?

About how the people of Westfield were 'heathens' and they had done something to him when he was a kid. I don't really remember

You lying sack of shit. You remember every word. Verbatim.

Exactly what he said. Mary Beth was in the bathroom and, when she came out, she mentioned something about us camping up here."

"Why didn't you say anything about this yesterday?" Mindy asked. Jonas was almost certain he could see steam coming out of her ears. He shrugged his shoulders, took a deep breath, and closed his eyes.

"The guy seemed harmless enough

Harmless... Like an axe murderer

I just figured he'd had too much to drink

All of his screws were loose and you fucking know it

I didn't really think about it too much after we got back."

Liar, liar pants on fire. You couldn't stop thinking about it. You still can't.

100

The group fell completely silent. Jonas opened his eyes and looked around the campfire. Everyone, it seemed, including Ryan and Whitney, were deep in thought. Jonas didn't think it wise to say anything else. He kept his mouth shut and waited for the next barrage of questions. When the questions didn't come, he hesitated but then opened his mouth to speak again.

"Seriously, guys. Nothing happened at all. It was blip on the radar. I'm sure Chris is

Dead

Just fine. Coral and Kevin are probably

Next

On their way back to town right now and Triple A will

Never even know we existed

Be coming down here soon to fix the tires. We'll all be

Brutally murdered before the weekend is over.

Right as rain before the end of the day."

Jonas stood from his spot and walked over to where Mindy was sitting. He leaned over and put a hand on her shoulder, giving it a little squeeze before kissing her on the top of her head. She looked up at him. He could see that, behind her angry exterior, she had the faintest speck of worry in her eye. She moved her hand up to his and squeezed it back, giving him a tight-lipped smile.

"Okay," She said, pushing up from her seat and clapping her hands once, "No use sitting around. Garrett, grab your skillet. Who wants some breakfast?"

Shortly after a very quiet breakfast of undercooked bacon and overcooked eggs fried over the campfire, Jonas glanced over and saw Garrett. He stood at the edge of camp, leaning against a tree, smoking a cigarette and staring out at the forest that spread out around them. His head was cocked like dog's, leaned towards the woods and the path leading back to what could only vaguely be described as civilization. As Jonas watched, Garrett paused, mid-drag on his cigarette and looked down at his watch.

It's like he thinks he's posing for the Marlboro Man calendar.

"When'd Cal scoot?" Garrett called over his shoulder. Ryan looked down at his watch.

"'Bout an hour or so ago," he responded as he slowly looked around the camp, the dawning realization that Cal had not yet returned slowly washing over him. Garrett took a drag off of his cigarette, lowered it to his side, and cocked his head towards the woods.

"D'ja hear th't?" He asked.

Now he's a fucking Indian guide?

The camp went silent as everyone paused to listed to what Garrett was hearing. Jonas leaned forward in his chair, straining his ears. He shrugged his shoulders.

"Hear what? I don't hear anything out of the ordinary," he said, answering for the group, "In fact, I don't hear anything at all." Garrett nodded and brought his cigarette back up to his lips to polish it off.

"S'actly whut I m'n," he stated, walking back to the circle and flicking his cigarette butt in the campfire, "Don' hea' no mot'r. Don' hea' nuth'n. Th'mean one'a two thangs: Cal done run outta gas… 'er sumpin' happ'n'd."

Like Lyle overtook him in the forest.

Or the Wackos of Westfield got him.

Either way, he's probably been brutally murdered by now.

Or he's being brutally murdered as we speak.

"It could just mean that they decided to take the quad all the way to town," Whitney suggested, trying to remain optimistic. If it hadn't been her cousin that had gone MIA, Jonas got the feeling that she wouldn't have said anything at all. Garrett shook his head.

"If'n it were jus' Cal, that' may'a b'n true, b' th' oth'r'ns know bett'r," Garrett replied. He took a could steps back to his leaning tree, staring down the road and into the brush, "They'd git theyselvesa maja league fine. Kev n' Core don'wanna deal wit'at." Garrett paused.

Gotta make sure to go for the dramatic effect.

"I'mma go walk down'a trail. See if'n I can't fin'im," Garrett said, turning back to the group, "Wanna gofa walk?" He motioned towards Jonas, who was caught completely off guard by the request.

No way.

If you say no, you're going to seem stand-offish.

Nope.

Mindy wants you to get along with him.

No way in hell.

Especially this weekend.

I don't want to be forced into more awkward small talk than is absolutely necessary.

Do it for her.

No fucking way.

"Joe-nass," Garrett asked again. Jonas cringed at the pronunciation of his name.

No thanks. I'm good.

"Sure," Jonas said, rising slowly from his chair, "Let's go check it out." Garrett gave the slightest nod of his head and plodded off towards the dirt path. Jonas, already regretting his decision, leaned over and kissed Mindy. She kissed him back and gently grabbed his wrist.

"Be nice," She whispered.

Do I really have a choice?

"I will," Jonas muttered, "Don't wait up." He turned away from the circle and jogged off to catch up with Garrett. As he approached, Garrett paused to light a cigarette. Jonas looked over his shoulder.

"Hey, now that we're away from the group," Jonas said, initiating small talk as he pulled his own pack of smokes from his pocket, "Do you think Cal's okay?" Garrett shrugged.

"I'ope so," He said as they left the field and entered the woods.

Into the Woods

The woods, which, when viewed from the relatively safe confines of the car, had been creepy during the day and absolutely horrifying at night, were even worse on foot. Jonas' eyes flitted back and forth, every shadow tugging on his already nervous stomach. His brain kept coming back to scenes from The Legend of Sleepy Hollow. He wasn't even aware how fast he was sucking down his cigarette until he got a mouthful of burning filter instead of smoke. He dropped his cigarette to the ground and snuck a glance over his shoulder, half expecting to see the Headless Horseman charging through the thick brush, flaming pumpkin in his hand as he descended upon them.

Would the Hessian be better or worse than an army of Westfield natives?

It may be a quicker demise.

They had been walking through the woods for a solid ten minutes before Jonas suddenly realized just how deafening the silent woods surrounding him actually were. He couldn't ever remember a time in his life when anything had been this quiet. He felt as though he could hear his blood coursing through his veins.

I don't think it's supposed to sound like this.

It's like the birds just up and left town.

That's probably because they can sense the impending doom that lies ahead.

For the love of God, you need to stop.

"I jes' wan'cha t'know, I got no intchins wit' Dee," Garrett said, completely out of left field. Jonas jumped at the sound of his voice, feeling as though he had been the victim of a verbal hit and run. He opened his mouth to retort but had literally nothing to say in response to that. He closed his mouth and nodded instead. Garrett nodded back and picked up Jonas' slack in the conversation, "I invit'd 'er t'th' weddin' as a pal. I din' re'lize sh'dun got a new fella n'er life."

Jonas still had nothing to say. He nodded again.

And suddenly I'm a fucking bobblehead.

"Jes' wan'ya t'kno, tha'sall," Garrett continued, "Dee n' me bin pals fer a longass time. I know'd th' invite got t'ya. C'nt blame ya'. I'da bin piss'd, too."

"I appreciate that," Jonas said, finally managing to hotwire his own vocal cords and finding the words that had somehow managed to get lost between his brain and his mouth. He felt like he should probably apologize to Garrett for something, but he wasn't exactly sure what he was supposed to apologize for.

How about for being a prick this entire time?

Maybe for being a judgmental asshole?

What about for being an untrusting shit for brains?

Actually, you should probably apologize to Mindy for that one.

Jonas opted to say nothing at all. The two walked on for a few feet with the awkward and uncomfortable silence engulfing them. As they passed by the abandoned camper, Jonas opened his mouth to say something, anything, if only to create some noise.

Before the words could bubble over his lips, Garrett stopped and put a hand out, pointing ahead of them.

"Looks like m' secon' choice was th' right 'n," He said. Jonas only had a moment to follow Garrett's finger before Garrett took off running towards Cal's body. Then Jonas was hot on his heels.

I don't wanna be left alone out here.

Accident

As the approached, Cal pushed himself up off of the tree he had been leaning on and began limping down the dirt path towards them. Jonas could see that the majority of his left leg was almost completely covered in a crimson hue.

"Y'okay, bud?" Garrett called out as they neared. Cal nodded his head and wiped a trickle of blood from his forehead.

"I'm fine," Cal muttered.

"What the hell happened?" Jonas asked, looking past Cal down the road, "Where are Kevin and Coral?"

They're dead.

Completely dead.

Dead, dead, dead.

"They got out on the road," Cal said, looking down at the wound in his leg, "They're on their way back to town right now."

"Well, that's a relief," Jonas sighed. Garrett gave Jonas a quizzical look and Jonas added quickly, "Because that's what I said to everyone back at camp." Garrett nodded and returned his attention back to Cal. Jonas looked the kid over, fully taking him in. He had been through the ringer. His hands and arms were scratched all to hell and the blood from the wound on his leg and the gash on his head had somehow managed to get everywhere on his body. It was caked on his shirt, matted in his hair, spritzed across his face.

He looks like a god damned tampon.

Real classy.

"Where's th' quad?" Garrett asked. Cal didn't take his eyes off of his leg as he jerked a thumb over his shoulder. Jonas noticed that the cuts on Cal's hands were deeper than he had initially thought.

Even if this weekend goes completely back to normal, I'm never getting on that fucking machine.

It's a goddamned death mobile.

"I was driving too fast. I lost control and clipped a tree," Cal mumbled. Jonas could hear a slight note of irritation in his voice, but he wasn't sure if it was because of his lack of skill as a four wheeler operator or the sheer feeling of stupidity for having crashed it at all, "I flipped the stupid thing and couldn't upright it."

"How far down is it?" Jonas asked.

"Just around the bend there," Cal replied. Garrett walked past him.

"Le's git'er n' head back," He said. Jonas followed him and Cal limped quickly after him. He came up alongside Jonas with his head bowed.

"I guess going to Gein's house is out of the question," He said. Jonas nodded his agreement and saw Cal's shoulders droop even further, deflating further into the air of defeat, "Damn. I really wanted to see that shit. He's a fascinating dude."

Why go see ol' Eddie when we have a traveling troupe of killers coming at us live and in person?

109

We've got front row tickets to a real life slaughterfest right here, right now!

"He was definitely fascinating," Jonas said as he picked up the pace to round the bend and catch up to Garrett. He wasn't particularly in the mood to talk with Cal about serial killers at the present time. All he wanted to do was head back to camp, pack up, get the hell out of here, and never look back.

"A'ight. This'ere's gon' be a team eff'rt," Garrett said as they came upon the upside-down four-wheeler. He pointed across from him to the opposite end of the quad, "Joe-nass, you lif'er, mma pull'er, n' we's gon' have'r on 'er feet in a jif. G'won 'ree."

The quad's a woman?

She might be the ugliest woman I've ever seen.

Jonas crouched down beside the four-wheeler, complying with Garrett's direction. He braced himself as Garrett counted to three and, when Garrett got there, he heaved with all his might. The quad flipped over almost instantly, landing on its wheels with a heaving bounce.

Maybe she is a woman after all.

"That was way easier than I anticipated," Jonas noted.

"Yup. Sh'aint that heavy," Garrett replied, itching his eyebrow, "Jes awkw'd."

Honestly, if Cal hadn't banged himself up, he probably could've done that himself.

Garrett turned away from the quad and gave a sharp whistle of admiration as he noticed the tree that Cal had slammed in to.

"Jaysus Crimn'y," He said, pointing at the broken sapling before him, "Ya pull'd a numb'r on tha' sumbitch." Jonas leaned in and looked closer. The bark of the tree had been torn back completely and the sapling was cracked and bent. A smear of blood ran across it and continued on to the tree beside it.

"You're lucky you didn't break your fucking leg," Jonas said distantly. Cal nodded.

"I know it. Damn lucky," He replied. He looked over his shoulder, back up the road towards camp, "Can we get back now? I'm starving."

Custer Had a Plan

"I think it's time for us to head out and look for Chris," Ryan said in a hushed voice, glancing back at the rest of the campers who were sitting around the fire. Even though they were several yards away, his words were barely audible at just over a whisper. It was the same way that everyone had been talking all day. Almost as though everyone was afraid that, if they spoke too loudly, this nightmare excursion would inevitably become worse.

It makes me wonder what would happen if I just started yelling.

Or screaming.

It just may come to that.

"You're probably right," Jonas murmured back.

The group had sat around the campfire all day in almost complete silence, speaking only when absolutely necessary. Every time a branch broke in the forest or the wind rustled the leaves on the trees, they all looked around at the woods simultaneously, expectant looks on their faces. After a while, the silence overtook them and, although no one would come right out and say what Jonas knew was on everyone's minds, one by one, they started to give up hope. Jonas finally had to get up and do something, so he and Ryan had opted to go together to procure some more wood for the fire.

Daylight was fast becoming twilight and dusk would be hurriedly approaching after that. Coral and Kevin had yet to arrive back from town, though that wasn't entirely surprising considering the distance they had to cover on foot. Everyone agreed that they may not make it back until well after nightfall, especially considering that they may have to hoof it again on their return trip if they couldn't find a ride. The fact that Chris had yet to make a triumphant return, on the other hand, was troublesome.

Chris is never coming back.

Ryan knew it.

You knew it, too.

Right from the get go.

Ryan had been right. After last night's incident at the bar, it was just a little too coincidental that Chris had just suddenly up and disappeared. On the same night that the car's tires had been slashed. Jonas had been holding out hope that there was a truly logical explanation for all of the events that had taken place. Maybe it was just a strange chance that all three events had happened on the same night. Maybe it was just some bored teenagers who were angry at the world and decided to pull a prank by slashing the tires. Maybe Chris was just gallivanting around the woods by himself and had completely lost track of time.

Maybe Lyle and the Westfield Heathens joined forces to fuck with you.

Regardless, I just hope that Kevin and Coral hustle their asses back. I don't want to spend another night in this Godforsaken place.

Kevin and Coral aren't coming back.

113

They'll be back.

They're in the same boat that Chris is in. You know, the one that travels across the river Styx.

They'll be back.

Admit it. You know that they're not coming back either.

Yes they are. They'll be back soon.

Denial ain't just a river in Egypt.

"If we're gonna do it," Jonas whispered, grabbing a few more pieces of firewood, "Let's do it now. While there's still some sun left in the sky." Ryan nodded his agreement and, with the firewood cradled in their arms, they started back towards camp. When they got back, Jonas tossed his pile in with the other wood before he walked over and stood by Mindy's chair. When she looked up at him, he saw the faintly glowing embers of hope in her eyes.

"Any sign of him?"

Jonas shook his head and the embers in her eyes faded away. She had lost everything, every last speck, of hope that Chris was coming back of his own accord. She lowered her blank eyes to stare straight ahead at the slowly dying fire. Ryan placed some wood on top to keep it going.

It sure would've been nice if someone had thought to bring some fluorescent bulbs.

And maybe four walls and a ceiling.

"Where's Narissa?" Ryan asked, moving away from the fire to stand next to Whitney. She motioned towards the tents.

"She went to lay down," Whitney replied. Jonas noticed that her voice was almost as blank as Mindy's gaze. She seemed lost. Somewhere far, far away from here in the realm of dreams.

This is well beyond the land of dreams.

This is a fucking nightmare.

"Ryan and I were just discussing," Jonas said, lowering his voice even further so as not to wake Narissa, "We're going to go look for Chris."

"Tha'sth' bes' idear I've heard all day," Garrett said, standing from his chair and grabbing his flashlight.

"We'll be back in a little while," Jonas said, leaning in to kiss Mindy on the cheek. Mindy pushed him away and got to her feet.

"I'm coming with," She stated. Whitney pushed herself up and walked to take her place at Mindy's side.

"Me too."

"We can handle it," Ryan assured them, "You don't have to come." Mindy shook her head.

"I'm sure you can," She said firmly, "But that doesn't change the fact that I'm coming with. Chris was my friend and I've been sitting around all day, worried sick. I have to do something." Jonas could tell by the tone of her voice that there was no use arguing with her. When she got it in her mind to do something and put her foot down, it stayed down. It was one of the reasons he loved her. It was also one of the reasons he hated her.

"You're staying here," Whitney informed Cal, who was struggling to get out of his chair and get to his feet. He had a

115

bandana tied around his leg where his wound was. Cal looked at Whitney with teenage rage in his eyes and opened his mouth to argue but Whitney held up a hand to silence him, "You can barely stand, let alone walk." She paused for a second, choosing her next words very carefully, "Besides, we need someone to stay here and keep an eye on Narissa."

"Also, I don't want to stay here alone, Cal," Mary Beth jumped in, motioning towards her flip-flops, "I wish I could assist, but I didn't bring the right shoes for trampling through the woods at night."

Besides, this isn't glamorous enough for the likes of you, Mary Beth.

It's certainly no Detroit.

We wouldn't want you to break a sweat.

Just sit down and take a load off.

Cal plopped miserably back into his seat, crossing his arms over his chest and commencing to pout. No one even bothered to pay him any mind.

"How are we going to do this?" Whitney asked. Jonas pulled his flashlight from his pocket and clicked it on.

"For starters, we stay within earshot of one another," he said, "We'll start by checking where he went to take a piss last night and work our way out from there."

"Sounds like a plan," Ryan said. Jonas looked around the circle in the ever fading light.

Yeah? Custer had a plan. Look where he ended up.

"Let's get moving."

116

Found

This is absolutely ridiculous.

All we're doing is putting ourselves on a nice, silver platter for these lunatics.

We should've done this earlier.

We should've waited until tomorrow morning.

We should just forget about him.

It's not like he's getting any deader.

They had been searching the forest for a good half and hour already and, thus far, they had come up with nothing but trees and mud in their flashlight beams. They had decided to stay within twenty feet of each other, give or take, leaving enough room for them to pan out and yet still be seen and heard by everyone else.

Yeah, everyone including the natives.

There are no natives.

There are and they're getting restless.

There are not.

They're watching you right now.

There's no one out there.

Oh yes there is. They're just waiting to strike.

Shut up.

Who do you think is next on the chopping block?

Stop it.

Chris, Kevin, Coral. Who's up to bat?

Shut the fuck up.

You're not going to find him. You know why?

Because he was already taken by the heathens?

No, because your idea was a terrible one. You're worthless.

Jesus.

Isn't that what this entire camping trip has boiled down to?

No. It started out as camping. Now it's about surviving.

Which you won't be doing because you're going to fuck this up.

What are you talking about?

You came on this trip to prove you're not worthless.

Not true.

You didn't want to leave Mindy alone with Garrett.

Wrong.

You didn't want her to realize that you're a mistake.

I came because I needed ideas for the new book.

Because your first book flopped?

Because I'm on a deadline.

Flopped.

I'm done with this.

Just face facts: You're no Doug.

What the fuck does that even mean?

Doug would have come out as the hero.

Stop it.

Doug wouldn't have let three people get killed.

Shut up.

Doug wouldn't have led the rest of the group out into the forest to meet their demise.

SHUT THE FUCK UP!

A chill ran down Jonas' spine like a finger on a xylophone. It was too quiet. He hadn't been paying attention and he had walked too far. He was out of earshot. He was out of sight. He was all alone. Was he alone? Were they all alone? What if they weren't. What if someone was out here? Had he walked his friends into the belly of the beast? He opened his mouth to call out to the rest of the group, to tell them they should all turn back, but before he had a chance to even make a sound, the ground dropped out from under him. He tried to stop himself, reaching out with flailing hands to grab hold of something to stop his fall, but it was too late. The ravine had appeared out of nowhere in the darkness. Now Jonas felt himself falling down the rabbit hole.

Doug would've seen the ravine.

Jonas landed on the ground below with a thud. The air was slammed out of his lungs and a flash of blinding white commandeered his vision for a moment. He squeezed his eyes shut, mentally taking inventory of his senses and thanking the Gods above that he had landed with only a thud and not a wet snap. He gave his breath a chance to catch up and, when it did, he sucked it down into his lungs in hefty gulps. He lay completely still on his back, regaining control of himself and allowing the white light to fade back to the darkness he had become accustomed to. Once it was as calm as he figured he could possibly hope for, he opened his eyes.

And came face to face with Chris.

He looked at Chris for a few seconds, his brain unable to make sense of the fact that he was lying beside Chris out here in the woods. Then he had a split second where he started to mentally celebrate the fact that he had succeeded in finding Chris. Then he recoiled in horror as his mind finally caught up and he noticed that Chris' glazed eyes weren't responding to the beam from Jonas' flashlight that was illuminating his pallid face.

I told you Chris was dead.

He must've fallen in the ravine. Just like I did.

So, you're the lucky one now?

Exactly.

You've never been the lucky one.

What?

When you're ship comes in, you'll be at the airport.

What do you mean?

Look closer.

Jonas scrambled over to pick up the flashlight from the ground where it had landed after the fall. Gripping the flashlight tightly, he moved in slowly towards Chris' body. He felt his heartbeat quicken when he noticed the caked blood and matted hair. His entire body broke out in a cold sweat when the flashlight beam landed on the hatchet that was embedded in Chris' skull. Jonas turned his head away and threw up the minimal contents that had been in his stomach.

What the fuck?

Chris isn't just dead. He was murdered.

Maybe he was just walking and...

And what?

He fell?

And landed on his head?

On a hatchet?

Wake up and smell the crime scene.

Chris was murdered.

Before Jonas could form another thought, a shrill shriek split the night.

Confusion Sets In

Jonas scrambled up the dirt wall of the ravine just as the second shriek came, so close on the heels of the first that Jonas couldn't tell if it was the same person screaming, overlap, or an echo.

That's coming from the camp.

Mary Beth probably needs some attention.

Jonas took off running, full tilt, through the woods towards camp as soon as he crested the ravine. It was damn near impossible to see where he was going and he stumbled over some bare roots, hoping that he was headed in the right direction. It had been hard enough to manage to walk carefully through the woods, slowly and with a flashlight. Now he was running, hoping that he wouldn't end up in another pit meeting the same demise as Chris. He felt his shirt catch and then tear as it was snagged by some low hanging branches. One slapped him across the face, leaving a stinging welt, but he barely even noticed. He caught a glimpse of light through the trees ahead of him and he pushed himself just a little harder. He burst through the trees at the edge of camp and found himself behind Mary Beth's hulking, silhouetted form. His eyes flitted back and forth across the campground as he approached the fire.

"Mary Beth," Jonas called out breathlessly as he worked to catch his breath, "What the fuck is going on? Where's Cal?" He glanced down at Mary Beth as he came around to face her.

Oh my fucking God.

Jonas stumbled backwards, moving away from Mary Beth but unable to take stop staring at her. Mary Beth's was staring back at him, eyes wide with terror. Her mouth was moving rapidly but no words were coming out. The only sound was a raspy, wet wheeze. She held out her hands, which had been pressed against her throat, to Jonas. Jonas' eyes grew to match Mary Beth's as he watched the blood pour from her neck down the front of her shirt. The slash across her throat made her look like a giant, macabre Pez dispenser. More blood seeped from her mouth, dribbling down her chin and dripping onto the blanket that was spread across her lap.

Holy merciful Mother of fuck!

Jonas took another lurching step backwards and his foot caught in the legs of one of the folding chairs. He fell backwards, landing on his left arm, just a few inches from the firepit, and he quickly fought to untangle himself from the chair. He scurried backwards like a crab, away from the grisly scene before him, until his hand landed in something wet. Something warm. Something tacky. He tore his eyes away from Mary Beth and looked down at where his hand was resting on the ground. It was resting on the blade of the machete. Both his hand and the blade were covered with blood.

"What the fuck is…" Ryan was yelling as he emerged from the tree line with the rest of the campers behind him. He stopped short when he saw Mary Beth and put his arm up to stop Whitney from running past him. Mindy came up on his other side and her jaw dropped. Whitney started to scream.

"Holy shit," Garrett said from somewhere off to Jonas' left. Jonas looked up at him from the ground and saw that Garrett's gaze was not on Mary Beth but on something behind Jonas. Jonas turned his head to see what Garrett was looking at. Narissa's tent. The door was slashed and torn with blood spattering the canvas. A form, Jonas could only assume that it was Narissa, lay halfway out on the grass. Jonas felt the earth tilt beneath him and he pulled his eyes away from Narissa's lifeless body.

And just like that, things have gone from bad to worse.

Everyone was looking at him now.

"Where the fuck is Cal?" Whitney screamed in a voice so shrill that Jonas didn't recognize it right away.

"I don't know," Jonas muttered, shaking his head. He started to get to his feet but Ryan barreled across the campground and slammed into him, grabbing the shoulder of Jonas' shirt and holding a forearm across his chest, pinning him to the ground. Jonas furrowed his eyebrows and held his hands up at his sides as best he could, "What the fuck are you doing, man?"

"Why are you here?" Ryan yelled, pulling Jonas a few inches off the ground and shoving him back down again. His forearm slipped up, jamming itself against the bottom of Jonas' throat. Jonas shook his head.

Because you had something to prove.

"I came running when I heard the screams," Jonas choked, "Just like you fucking did."

"Bullshit," Ryan shouted, "You weren't out in the fucking forest with us, otherwise we would've gotten here at the same fucking time."

You weren't out in the forest?

Where were you, Jonas?

"Yes I was," Jonas croaked. He stared at Ryan with confusion in his eyes. He had almost forgotten about his discovery in the woods after seeing the crime scene that had been waiting for him when he got back to camp. Now it came rushing back to the forefront of his mind. He struggled to pull in a gulp of air, "I found Chris." Mindy's hands shot to her mouth in a poor attempt to hide the gasp that escaped her lips.

"Is he…" She asked, unable to finish the question before her voice cracked. Jonas did his best to nod.

"He's dead."

Tell them he fell in a hole and managed and used his skull to soften the blow from the hatchet.

"Oh, you found Chris?" Ryan snarled, the anger rising in his voice like a tea kettle, "Why the fuck didn't you call for us?"

Why didn't you call for them?

"It all happened so fast," Jonas replied, "I fell in a hole and Chris was at the bottom."

"He fell in a hole?" Mindy asked, "That's how he died?"

I told you your story wouldn't hold up.

It's not a story.

"No, I fell in a hole," Jonas stated, "Chris was at the bottom… he had… he had a…"

125

Now even you are having a hard time buying what you're selling.

Shut up.

"He had a what?" Ryan growled, pressing down harder on Jonas' throat. Jonas winced.

"He was murdered," Jonas croaked. Ryan gave Jonas' windpipe another hard shove as he scrambled off of him. Jonas rolled over to his side, wheezing in a mouthful of dirt and ashes. He moved his bloody hand up to his neck to rub his throat. Coughing and gasping for air, he slowly got to his feet. He looked at Mindy, who was shaking her head, and took a step towards her. She shrank back and Jonas cocked his head.

Now you've gone and done it.

"You stay away from me," Mindy whispered.

Here it comes.

"What?" Jonas wheezed.

"You're crazy," Mindy said, her voice staying the same volume, "Stay away from me."

They're on to you.

"What are you talking about?" Jonas asked, unsure if he was directing the question towards Mindy or his inner monologue. Ryan stepped between Jonas and Mindy.

"You killed them all, you son of a bitch," Ryan growled. Jonas shook his head.

Why the fuck would they think I killed them?

C'mon, Jonas, they've already got you. Fess up.

"What?" Jonas said, "No I didn't." He could feel the vein pulsing, throbbing behind his left eye. He felt a massive headache just laying in wait as he tried to catch up, to get on the same page as the rest of them.

Are you sure you didn't kill anyone?

"Mindy, tell them I was with you last night," Jonas pleaded. Mindy stood in silence for a moment before she shook her head.

"We didn't go to sleep together," Mindy mumbled. Jonas furrowed his eyebrows.

The hits just keep on coming.

"What the hell are you talking about?"

"I got in the tent and you said you were going to go brush your teeth," Mindy said, "I must've fallen asleep. I don't remember you coming to bed."

Sounds like you need an alibi.

"Is that when you killed him, you sick fuck?" Ryan snarled. His hands clenched into fists at his sides.

Is that when you killed him?

No!

So you killed him later?

I didn't kill him!

Then where the fuck were you?

"I went to brush my teeth!" Jonas shouted.

Did you? Did you really?

YES!

You don't have to convince me. I don't care either way.

"Is that why you didn't want us to go looking for Chris earlier?" Whitney asked.

More incriminating evidence.

Everything is pointing towards you.

Say goodnight, Gracie.

"You didn't want to go look for Chris earlier?" Mindy asked, looking at Jonas in disbelief. Jonas shook his head,

"I just didn't want to get

Caught

Everyone all worked up," Jonas said, trying to keep his composure. He felt his heart thudding against his ribcage.

"Or did you just think you would get away with it?" Ryan snapped. Before Jonas even had time to fully process the events that were unfolding before him, Ryan was advancing on him, "Were you going to kill us next? Is that why you decided to lead us into the woods? Or was it so you could double back and take care of the loose ends?"

What was the batting order?

Who was on deck?

How did you decide?

"I didn't kill anyone," Jonas stated, standing his ground.

Right?

I don't know. You tell me.

Ryan's already clenched fist shot out and connected with the side of Jonas' jaw. Jonas reeled backwards, falling on his ass once again. Ryan took two steps forward and loomed over him, pointing fervently at the machete on the ground beside them.

"That's yours," Ryan spat.

He has a point. You do own a machete.

It was brought for camping... so I could get in touch with my mountain man side. Ryan has...

"Wait a minute," Jonas said, his mind still reeling from the sucker punch that Ryan had thrown. His confusion was starting to wane, replaced by anger. He saw the red creeping into his vision from his periphery, "How the fuck can you be so sure? You have one of those, too."

Oh, turning the tables on him.

Well played.

Can you keep it going?

Ask the next logical question.

"How do we know you're not the fucking killer?" Jonas asked. Ryan scoffed at the very idea and looked around the circle for back-up. Jonas followed his gaze. He could see the hesitation in their eyes.

You planted the seed of doubt.

Their over-taxed minds aren't easily swayed.

Especially considering there's a serial killer on the loose.

Ryan doesn't like being in your shoes.

"My machete is in the car," Ryan said. Jonas could hear the defensive tone in his voice.

You've got him on the ropes.

Don't let him off that easy.

"Prove it," Jonas said. Ryan's lips pulled back in a menacing grimace. He opened and closed his fists, ready to pounce on Jonas and tear him limb from limb.

That wouldn't really help him prove his innocence.

It wouldn't do you a whole hell of a lot of good either.

Ryan continued to stare Jonas down for a few moments, as if trying to decide the best course of action.

"That's not a problem," he stated. Turning to Garrett, he pointed a finger down at Jonas, "Watch him."

"Uh-huh," Garrett grunted. Ryan strode across the campground to pull open the passenger door of the black Ford Explorer. He leaned inside, keeping his eyes on Jonas the entire time, as though he expected him to bolt to his feet and continue his killing spree, "My machete is right..." Ryan's voice trailed off. He turned his attention away from the group and started rustling around in his car.

The hunter has become the game.

Well played, sir.

"It was right fucking here," Ryan said, his voice muffled from inside the car. It was just on the precipice of going from calm to frantic. He popped back up out of the car and turned towards Jonas, eyes blazing, "You took it, you bastard. You're trying to pin this on me."

He puts on a hell of a show. I'll give him that.

Either that or he's officially lost his mind.

"I didn't take your machete," Jonas roared back, "I told you, I didn't kill anybody." He got back to his feet, moving towards

130

Ryan, ready to verbally assault him. Then he caught a glimpse of something in the back of the Explorer. Just a brief hint of movement. A shadow. Jonas squinted his eyes, trying to get a better look. The shadow appeared again, followed by a quick glint of silver as something metallic caught the glow of the campfire. All of the anger within Jonas' body turned to dust and was replaced by fear. His eyes went wide.

I guess you were innocent all along.

"Ryan, get the fuck out of the way!"

Ryan's eyes went wide at the sound of Jonas' voice. Instinctively, he lunged forward, away from the car, just as a silver blade dropped down like a guillotine and landed against the door behind him. The machete fell to the ground, landing on the ground leaning against the running board of the open door. Whitney screamed. Ryan tried to turn around, to make his way to Whitney, but his momentum carried him forward. He was off balance to begin with but, when his feet tangled up in one of the ropes that held down Narissa's tent, that was all she wrote. His upper body pitched forward as his legs came to a screeching halt, tethered together by the taught rope, and he fell. His forehead connected with the seat of the picnic table and bounced off of it like a basketball with a sickening thump. A fine spray of blood shot across the table from the gash in his head, coating the food that had been left out in a mist of crimson. Ryan didn't even have a chance to utter a yelp of pain before his body crumpled to the ground in a heap.

Well, that didn't look like any kind of fun at all.

Should we help him?

"Ryan!" Whiney shrieked, running full speed to where his body lay motionless on the ground. She fell to her knees at his side and grabbed him by the shoulders, immediately beginning to shake him. He didn't respond. Jonas started to walk slowly towards her. From the corner of his eye, he could see Garrett doing the same. Both of them keeping their eyes on the car.

For a minute there, I thought I was the only one who saw that.

Because everyone else is blind?

"Whitney," Jonas whispered, watching the fire reflect off of the machete in the car's doorway, "You have to get away from the car before…"

Too fucking late.

The shadow from the backseat emerged from the darkness in the passenger doorway. The person slid out from within the inky black, ever so slowly, and stood beside the open door. It reached out and wrapped a hand around the machete's handle. Jonas froze.

"Whitney," Jonas hissed, trying not to draw the person's attention to him or to Whitney. But Whitney was in her own world, one that only had room for her and for Ryan. Jonas heard the slow, metallic grating sound as the blade of the machete ran across the car's running board. The shadow had picked it up.

There's not much time.

You need to get her moving.

He stared at the shadow. It was standing motionless beside the car and, from what Jonas could tell, it looked like it was facing away from them. It appeared to be examining the blade of the machete. If he could just get to Whitney or get Whitney to come to him before the shadow turned around, he would be in the clear. He just had to make sure not to draw it's attention.

"Whitney, run!" Mindy shrieked.

Fuck.

The shadow straightened up and began to turn slowly towards Whitney. It started with the head and then the rest of the body followed. With a slow, lurching step, it was on the move.

It has it's next victim locked in.

Who the fuck is that lunatic?

What the fuck is it?

Jonas decided that, at the present time, he didn't care to find out. He bounded forward, covering the short distance that was left between himself and Whitney in just a few steps. Garrett, whose legs were longer, arrived at the same time. As if they had rehearsed this on more than one occasion, Garrett grabbed Whitney by her upper arm and yanked her to her feet. She started to sink back to her knees again, but Garrett held her up. Jonas slid to his knees on the ground beside Ryan and took hold of his collar.

He's still breathing.

If you don't get out of here in a hurry, that's going to end abruptly for all of you.

Jonas chanced a glimpse at the shadow. It was rapidly approaching. The machete raised above its head. A few more steps and it had them.

Garrett pulled the catatonic Whitney back across the campground towards the frozen Mindy. Her feet didn't move properly and the two of them almost stumbled into the fire. The stumble must've jarred something loose in Whitney's brain

134

because, at the last second, she got her feet moving properly and was able to keep herself from falling. Garrett held her hand to steady both her and himself. Jonas heard the faint whistling of the downward descent of the machete's blade. Without any further hesitation, Jonas gripped Ryan's collar tight and yanked him backwards, away from the machete wielding maniac. The blade made a dull chopping sound as it buried itself deep in the ground where Ryan had been laying.

This is like a marathon of horror movie hellscapes.

Jonas readjusted his grip on Ryan's collar and, getting to his feet and turning around, he dug in his heels to move forward, dragging the lifeless body of his friend across the campsite towards his three companions. He could tell, without even looking back, that the shadow was already on the move. It was moving slowly, but it was still coming for them nonetheless. A cold sweat broke out over his face.

How far away is he?

Don't think about that, just move.

After what seemed like an eternity, Jonas reached the other side of the campfire and immediately let go of Ryan. He sucked in a deep breath of air and tried not to focus on the burning muscles that he clearly hadn't used in a very long time.

That dude needs to join a gym.

We don't have time for this right now.

Jonas turned around to look back at the shadow. It was still lurching towards them. They had put some distance between themselves and the maniac, but they needed to keep moving if they wanted to keep that distance. Jonas leaned down and grabbed Ryan's left arm. He pointed at Garrett.

"Grab the other one," He barked, but Garrett was moving before Jonas had even opened his mouth. Together, they pulled the unconscious bulk from the ground, holding him between them as though he were nothing more than a drunken marionette. Jonas nodded his head towards the poll barn, "In there. Everyone. Now."

What are you going to do when you get in there?

You still have no phones, no wheels, and no plan.

We'll think of something.

That terrifies me.

Mindy grabbed Whitney by the hand and the two tore off towards the barn. Jonas and Garrett ran behind them, as fast as they could while lugging the dead weight of Ryan's body. Mindy threw open the door and Whitney bolted inside.

"Come on," Mindy shouted, "Hurry!" Jonas grunted in response.

Why don't you come sling this arm over your shoulder and see how fast you move?

It's a good thing that freakshow isn't moving that fast.

Have you glanced over your shoulder recently? How fast is he moving?

I'm going to gamble. I'm not turning around.

Garrett and Jonas reached the door and Jonas released Ryan, transferring the full weight to Garrett. Mindy was holding the door open for them. Garrett entered the barn and pulled Ryan in after him. Jonas chanced a look behind them. The shadow was still a ways off but he was definitely headed in their general direction.

Slow and steady wins the race.

He grabbed Mindy by the elbow and saw her wince. With his adrenaline this amped, he hadn't been aware of how hard he had grabbed her. He eased his grip and looked her in the eye.

"Did you put the padlock on the outside of the garage door to this place?" He demanded.

"I… I think so," Mindy nodded. Jonas shook his head urgently and squeezed her arm again.

"You can't guess," He snapped, "You have to know."

"Yes. I put the padlock on the garage door."

"And this is the only other door in or out?" He asked. Mindy nodded quickly. Jonas gritted his teeth, "Good."

He yanked Mindy close to him, pressing his lips to hers. He held her there for a moment, feeling the heat of her breath on his upper lip, before pulling away. He looked her in the eyes again.

"No matter what happens, remember that I'll always love you," He said, "Remember that." Mindy's eyebrows furrowed in confusion. Jonas didn't wait for any follow up questions. He shoved her through the doorway as hard as he could. Mindy yelped as her feet connected with Ryan's body and she fell over on top of him, reaching out to grab Garrett's arm for support and taking him down with her. They landed in a heap on the floor. Jonas had just enough time to see the surprised look on her face turn into one of surprised anger. Then he slammed the door.

He leaped over the box that held the firewood and, heaving his shoulder into it with all his might, he tipped it sideways. It fell forward, wedging itself between the door and one of the wooden posts holding up the tin awning, and stuck fast. Jonas plucked the padlock from the hook beside the door and snapped it shut on the bolt, locking the door from the outside. He could hear Mindy on the other side of the door, scrambling to her feet. She threw her body against the interior of the door.

She's stuck in there.

There's no way for her to get out.

There's also no way for that maniac to get in.

That means she's safe.

Now what?

Jonas turned to face the shadow, now just a few yards away. The machete was still held out at his side.

Now I get to prove to everyone that I'm worth a damn.

One More Fucking Plan

Jonas stood his ground, waiting, horrified, for just the right moment. The exact right moment.

You only get one shot at this, man.

Don't fuck this up.

I won't.

Wait for it.

Waaaaiiit for iiiit.

Closer.

Not yet.

I know what I'm doing.

NOW!

The shadow was almost on top of him. It brought the machete up over its head. Jonas reached out with his right hand and grabbed a thick piece of firewood. The machete came slashing down just as Jonas snapped the wood up in front of himself just in time. The blade stuck fast in the log and Jonas shoved the firewood forward, exerting extra energy with his left arm. The jarring motion threw the shadow off balance and Jonas jerked the wood back to the left. The machete was wrenched from the shadow's hand. As an added bonus that Jonas hadn't planned for, the right end of the log jerked forward and caught the shadow on the side of the face with a dull, hollow thump.

That's what a coconut sounds like.

Jonas stood still, waiting for the shadow to fall. It didn't happen. It reeled back a step and tottered from side to side for a moment, but then it stood, stock still. Jonas dropped the log and stepped back a few paces.

Time for a new plan.

Or an amended one.

Either way, back to the old drawing board.

Whatever you do, just hurry the fuck up.

The shadow brought it's hand up to it's face, shaking it's head, and took a step towards Jonas. As the maniac stepped into the moonlight, Jonas saw that he had knocked the shadow's black hood back. He could see the killer's face.

No fucking way.

There's no way in hell.

How the fuck can it be…

"Cal?" Jonas spat. The use of the name didn't seem even remotely feasible. Cal wasn't a killer. There was no way Cal could've killed all those people. He was a weird, obnoxious kid, yes. But a killer? Hardly. But Jonas watched, his brain reeling, as Cal slowly locked eyes with him. A smile slowly spread across Cal's lips. A layer of blood and saliva now covered his teeth. Jonas assumed that this was from the blow to the head with the log. With the blood on his teeth and his overly gigantic grin, Cal no longer looked like the stupid kid they had brought camping with them. He looked… off. Way off. The look of sheer insanity that was smoldering in his eyes, coupled with the grin that was stolen from the Cheshire Cat, and every ounce of doubt was washed away from Jonas' thoughts. Cal had most definitely killed all of those people.

140

He's a looney tune.

He's dangerous.

Come on, you can take him.

He's what? Sixteen years old?

He killed Mary Beth.

That probably wasn't that hard. It would've been like cutting up a marshmallow.

She probably had the same dexterity as a marshmallow.

He killed Narissa.

She was asleep and disoriented when he attacked her.

She was probably still half asleep when he cut her up.

He killed Chris.

He... Well, okay. I'll give you that one. Chris was a pretty rough and tumble dude.

He almost took out Ryan.

Okay, okay. I hear you... So, what's the plan?

We have to lead him away from the poll barn. We have to keep him occupied.

Until when?

Until help arrives.

Help? What help? You mean Kevin and Coral? Kevin and Coral are...

We don't know that for sure. Shut the fuck up about it.

Okay, do what you gotta do. Don't say I didn't warn you.

Jonas took one last look at Cal's psychotic transformation. Then he turned around and took off running towards the dirt road. He hoped Cal was following him.

Why aren't you moving faster? You have a murderer behind you, turn up the juice.

He's a murderer, yes, but he's a murderer with a limp. I need to stay just out of reach. But I still want him to think he can catch me.

The brain on you. Color me impressed.

The smile that had started to spread across Jonas' lips quickly faded. From behind him, he heard the unmistakable sound of a motor revving to life. He stopped in his tracks and spun around. A single headlight flared up from the darkness. The motor revved again and the headlight rushed forward. Towards him.

I'd like to retract my former statement.

Shit.

You forgot about the dirt bike.

I forgot about the dirt bike.

How could you forget about the dirt bike?

How could I forget about the dirt bike?

Well, Flo-Jo, we're gonna have to think of plan while we're en route.

Yeah.

Feet, do your thang.

Jonas wheeled back around and poured everything he had into his legs. He tore across the field, the muscles in his legs snapping like rubber bands and propelling him forward. From the sound of it, the bike behind him was closing in fast. He could hear, he could feel, the motor coming closer. He knew that it was only a matter of time before it was on top of him.

What are you going to do?

I don't know.

Probably should figure that out.

That's probably a good idea.

The bike was just behind him now. Jonas swore he could hear Cal cackling maniacally from behind the handlebars. He knew, just as well as Jonas did, that the jig was up. Then a flash of an idea illuminated in Jonas' head. Without thinking, he screeched to a halt and turned sharply to his right, tearing off in a b-line towards the trees. The bike flew past him, a swishing sound followed by Cal's voice letting loose a string of profanities as he went past. The bike took a wide berth and wheeled back around. By the time it was back on track, behind him, Jonas was already leaping from the field into the woods. He had managed to buy himself just a little bit of extra time. Albeit, it was not much, but every little bit helped.

He can't use the bike in here. Not at night, anyway.

Where are we headed?

We have to get to the abandoned camper.

Why?

I have a plan.

Custer had a…

I know, I know. Custer had a plan.

Jonas high-tailed it, running as fast as he could, forgetting about the exhaustion he should've been feeling, the thudding of his heart, the pain in his lungs. He dodged tree stumps and roots, low hanging branches and vines, as though he had them all mapped out. He felt a wave of exhilaration rush through his body. His adrenaline pushed him forward. No longer was he the city boy, disgusted by all that camping entailed. He was no longer Jonas the fuck up, Jonas the failure, Jonas the useless. He was just Jonas now, a Jonas stripped down to the barest of bare bones of the human psyche. He was the rarest earthen form that he had ever imagined himself being. He was this and, yet, he was so much more. Running through the woods, protecting his fair maiden, protecting those who he had realized were his tribe, all other thoughts had left his mind. He was Jonas the warrior. He ducked as a low hanging limb popped into his sight line and he spun to the right as a tree emerged in front of him in the darkness.

This is animal instinct at its finest.

He ran through the forest, listening to the sound of the dirt bike alongside the woods. Cal was atop it, waiting for Jonas to come back out from the trees so that he could play with him. Like an animal waiting for its prey. Jonas curved his path, running back towards the edge of the trees, seeing the beam headlight of the dirt bike speeding alongside it, just a few yards away. He couldn't see Cal's face, but he knew that Cal was scanning the forest, watching Jonas run to the edge of the woods. Waiting. Jonas let out an animal howl, a war cry, loud enough for Cal to hear over the deafening engine. As he reached the edge of the woods, Jonas turned sharply to his right, staying just inside the edge of the forest, waving his arms about his head wildly so that Cal could see him. That was exactly what Jonas wanted. He knew that, if he stepped one foot out of the canopy of trees that surrounded him, Cal would mow him down without a second's hesitation. He needed Cal to see where he was so that Cal would stay hot on his trail.

You got me in your sights, you sick, twisted bastard?

As if reading Jonas' thoughts, the bike's engine revved up even further and the bike leaped forward. Cal was riding the tree line, just alongside Jonas. Jonas looked straight ahead, not even bothering to glance at Cal. Cal was reaching the end of the line. A peninsula of trees jutted outward and forced the field to bottleneck into the dirt road. Jonas lowered his head, like a charging bull, and pushed himself forward even harder than he imagined he could. Cal fast approached the grove.

Now, here's where we get risky.

What's Cal gonna do?

Jonas happened a glance out of the corner of his eye as he entered the grove. The bike cut sharply to the left, just as Jonas hoped it would. He wanted to stop to see where Cal would head, to see if he would do what Jonas needed him to do. But he couldn't stop, even for a second, if he wanted this plan to work. He had to keep moving. If Cal did what he was supposed to do, then Jonas had just bought himself more time.

And that's going to make all the difference.

Jonas lost sight of the bike, but he immediately put it out of his mind. After a few moments, he erupted from the woods and found himself facing the back side of the abandoned camper. He raced around to the front door and grabbed the handle. He twisted it down and pulled but was not at all surprised to find it locked. He pulled his pocketknife from his jeans.

Good thing I'm a burgeoning criminal.

Mostly it's a good thing you pay attention when you talk to crime writers.

Jonas flipped open the saw-like blade. He vaguely recalled being told once that it was used to descale fish, but he wasn't entirely certain. Up until this point, the blade had been a useless feature on the knife. Jonas jammed it into the lock and wiggled it around, applying pressure to the doorknob.

This isn't going to work.

It's not going to work.

It's not going to...

The tumbler inside the lock gave way with a small click and the handle began to move freely. Under normal duress, Jonas would've taken a second to celebrate but, instead, he yanked the door open and closed the knife blade. He jammed the knife back into his pocket, settling for a small grin. There would be time to celebrate later, if he made it through.

Fish scaler, lock pick... In the end, what's the difference?

He jumped into the camper and slammed the door behind him.

The Last Stand

The stench of the interior of the camper socked Jonas in the face like a hit from Mike Tyson as he stepped inside. At first, he recoiled at the foul-smelling odor, gagging as his instinct nearly pushing him right back out the door. He stopped himself and pushed forward, knowing full well that he didn't have another option. He brought his hand up to cover his mouth and nose, partially to block the smell but also to stop himself from vomiting. He kept moving. The smell was overpowering, but it was nothing compared to the sight of the grisly bodies sprawled out before him on the camper's dingy floor.

I think I can safely say that I am certain what happened to Kevin and Coral.

What's left of them anyway.

Jonas tore his eyes away from the macabre, slashed corpses before him and scanned the camper for what he was looking for. When his eyes locked in on it, he stepped carefully over them, slipping a little in the

Oh my God... Did I just step on a piece of brain?

Blood and whatever other body parts were strewn about, and lunged for the stove. He reached out his hand, his fingers gripping hold of the knob. He pushed the knob in and spun it as far as it could go, all the way to the right. He reached out with his other hand and quickly did the same to all of the knobs on the stove. Once they were all on, full blast, he yanked open the oven door and repeated the process with the bigger knob on the top of the stove. He leaped back over the bodies and tore out the front door. He was just in time to see the flickering headlight of the dirt bike through the trees. It was tearing up the dirt path.

The son of a bitch took the bait.

I gotta get moving or this was a completely pointless undertaking.

Jonas jumped down the couple of steps from the camper and hit the ground running. He moved to the front of the trailer and breathed a sigh of relief when he saw the propane tank locked onto the front bumper. He placed his hands on the knob and took another deep breath. He closed his eyes in a silent prayer.

Now, here's the real test: How full is this bad boy?

Only one way to find out.

He gripped the metal knob and strained to turn it. It wouldn't budge. For a split second, Jonas thought that the owners had accidentally left it on since their last visit. He dug in and twisted it harder, willing, with all his might, for it to move. He gritted his teeth and, suddenly, the knob loosened. With a small hiss of release, it began to turn.

"Thank you," He muttered and continued to spin it to the open position. It was slow going at first but, with each rotation, it became easier and easier. The faint whisper of gas as it started to flow through the ancient hose was like hearing the Mormon Tabernacle choir sing Hallelujah. Jonas began spinning the knob rapidly and, after a few more rotations, the whispering turned into a whooshing and the knob wouldn't turn any further. Jonas let go of the knob and gave another war cry as he ran back to stand in the camper's doorway.

At the sound of Jonas' call, Cal turned the dirt bike abruptly. The headlight washed over Jonas just as he set a foot on the step of the camper and Cal came barreling out of the woods. Jonas turned to face his attacker.

Cal jammed on the brakes and the bike came to screeching halt, kicking up dirt and rocks, in the middle of the small clearing around the camper. He threw his leg over the bike and let it fall to the ground, the engine still sputtering. Jonas wiggled his fingers at Cal.

"C'mon, ya fuck," Jonas bellowed, "You still looking for blood?" Cal didn't respond verbally but, in the glow of the headlight beam, he saw him nod his head slowly. He began to walk across the clearing.

What a fucking psycho.

As he neared the camper, Cal unsheathed the machete from its place on his belt. Jonas saw the glint of steel as the headlight caught the blade.

He must've taken a second to free it from the log.

Good on him… Knowing what's important.

Cal plodded forward, holding the machete at shoulder height off to his side. When he was just a few steps from the camper, almost at slashing range, Jonas spun around and leaped back inside. He heard the clang as the blade hit the doorframe behind him but he didn't bother turning around. He leaped over Kevin and Coral for the third time. Then, he stopped and turned back

149

around to face Cal. Cal was climbing through the door. Jonas stuck his hand in his pocket.

Give it a minute. Let him come closer.

You don't want to blow your load too early.

I know what I'm doing.

I know you do. You're a regular John McClane all of a sudden.

Yippee-kay-aye, motherfucker.

Cal didn't even attempt to step over the corpses as he moved towards Jonas. His sneaker pressed down on the middle of Kevin's back with a sickening, squelching noise. He dropped the machete to the ground as he walked the length of the camper and put his hand in his pocket, mirroring Jonas. When he removed his hand, Jonas heard a familiar click.

"That's my switchblade, you fucking asshole," Jonas growled.

"Don't worry," Cal whispered back, the corners of his mouth pulling up into a grin, "You'll have it back in a second. You don't have anywhere left to run." Cal took another step forward, a crunch from beneath his foot as he stepped on Coral's neck. He was no standing directly in front of Jonas, close enough so Jonas could smell his breath. Cal stopped and Jonas saw his nose twitch before he lowered his eyes. Jonas pulled his lighter from his pocket.

"That's exactly what you think it is," Jonas said. He flipped the top of his lighter open, "Tell you what, you can keep the knife. Don't say I never gave you nothing." Cal's eyes went wide. Jonas brought his thumb down across the lighter.

Doug wouldn't have done that.

Yeah... No shit.

The lighter sparked and gave birth to a beautiful golden flame.

Fireworks

Mindy's had just said to herself, in defeat, that this was going to be the last time she was going to throw herself at the door to the poll barn when her shoulder struck the sweet spot to the barn door. The wood box on the opposite side of the door was knocked askew just far enough for her to be able to push the door open wide enough to slip through. Once outside, she shoved the box aside and threw the door open wide. She moved her left hand to her shoulder, rolling it forwards and then backwards, knowing full well she was going to be in pain in the morning.

"Seriously. Guys, I'm fine now," Ryan mumbled. Mindy turned to see Garrett and Whitney assisting him through the open doorway. His head was still bleeding profusely, but he managed to shake the two off of his arms so he could lean against the doorjamb. The four campers looked around the darkened campground for some sign of Jonas. Or the killer.

"I don't see him," Mindy said. Garrett nodded, holding out his bandana to Ryan. Ryan took it and pressed it to the wound in his head.

"Don' see Cal ne'th'r."

The murky darkness of the woods just outside of Westfield, Wisconsin lay silent. The campers listened to the nothingness around them. There were no birds calling to one another. No owls hooting. The frogs and insects had muted their chirps and croaks. Even the wind in the trees seemed surprisingly absent.

There wasn't so much as a hushed sound of leaves rustling. The night was perfectly serene.

Until the fireball erupted in the distance.

The campers all leaped back. Ryan spilled over into the poll barn, Whitney and Garrett slammed into the tin wall, and Mindy started to tumble over the wood that had been strewn about the ground at her feet, but she managed to catch herself on one of the awning poles before she went down. They all stood still, stunned, staring at the explosion rocketing fire upwards into the black sky, blotting out the stars. A few seconds later, they heard the sound of shrapnel falling to Earth in the far corner of the field. Mindy sucked in a gasp of air and pushed herself off of the pole.

"Jonas," She whispered. Then she took off running across the field.

Garrett was only two steps behind her. Whitney helped Ryan back to his feet before the two of them began stumbling across the field as well. By the time they reached the dirt path, the fiery remains had ceased raining down and, when they reached the edge of the small clearing that had once been the abandoned camper's resting place, they found a charred, unrecognizable blazing mess in its place. Black plumes of smoke poured from the top of the fire.

Whitney let loose an animal screech. Mindy spun around to see what was happening behind her and she watched as Whitney stumbled backwards, hand over her mouth. Her feet couldn't keep up with the momentum of her upper body and she fell, landing flat on her ass. It didn't seem to faze her. Her feet kept scrabbling, pushing her away from the fire, and she raised her hand to point upwards. Mindy followed her finger to the tree beside the camper and her eyes climbed the side of the smoldering trunk to the charred remains of the limb that was overhanging what was left of the camper. From the limb, about fifty feet up, hung a lifeless, soot covered body. Even though it had been put through the ringer, Mindy recognized the tattered bandana tied around it's leg. They had found Cal.

Mindy swallowed the lump in her throat, looking away from Cal just as the ground began to spin. Darkness started to flood her line of vision. Somewhere, very far away, she heard Garrett's unmistakable twang calling her name. Then the ground was rushing up to meet her and everything faded to black.

The Calvary Arrives

"We're gonna need all the help we can get out here," Sherriff Cox said into the walkie. He opted that it was best to keep it short and simple. You never knew what knuckleheads were listening to scanners and would wind up just getting in the way. Besides, he was at a loss for words. He wasn't a man of many words in a normal situation and this situation wasn't normal by any stretch of the imagination.

His evening had consisted of the standard boredom that always filled the patrols in Westfield. He had been on a domestic call, a drunk yokel harassing an out of towner, when the call had come in. According to dispatch, some concerned citizen passing by had heard or seen an explosion just off of Bear Paw Road and had called it in. Cox figured that, if the motorist had been passing by just a minute before or after the explosion, they would've thought nothing of the enormous billows of smoke they were seeing and would've just chalked it up to stupid kids having a bonfire that had grown a bit too big as the night's drinking amped up. Unfortunately, the driver had impeccable timing.

Cox had been the first first responder and had immediately called for back up when he saw the remains of the kid in the tree. There was no quick way to deal with something of that nature, though he had been all set to write it off as some sort of horrible accident.

His second order of business, after calling for back up, had been to revive the poor girl who was passed out on the ground.

After a cursory glance around the three people standing around her, he figured it was just a wild, binge drinking party gone awry. This girl must've been a light weight. When he got her up and moving, he had gotten a better look at her face and took a second look, a harder one this time, at the rest of the group. That was when he realized this wasn't a crazy party. This was something much, much worse. He didn't know what yet but, based on the signs of crying, exhaustion, and trauma, he didn't want to know. Not just yet. He just hoped that his back-up would arrive soon.

Then he had started talking to the survivors.

The first thing the group told him was that there had been a murder. His ears perked up right away at the word. Then he realized there was an S at the end of that word. His body and brain immediately went on red alert. There weren't a lot of murders around these parts.

"You," Cox said, looking at the girl on the ground, "What's your name?"

"Mindy."

"You said there was a murder?" Cox grunted, "That how your buddy got up in the tree?"

"I don't know how he got up there," the girl, Mindy, replied. She was still kind of out of it, but Cox could tell that she was not drunk. Then she launched into a story that made Cox's flesh tingle. She filled him in on the few details she knew, her boyfriend's last words to her, him shoving her into the barn, snippets of conversation she could hear from just outside the barricaded door.

"He said it was Cal," Mindy said. Cox raised an eyebrow.

"Cal?" He repeated, "Who's Cal?"

"Cal's up…" The other girl in the group started to say, but her voice broke off and she started crying. A kid who was pretty banged up, bleeding from the forehead, put his arm around her and drew her close. She sobbed into his chest. Cox straightened up.

"Who are you?" He asked, pointing his pen at the banged-up guy.

"My name's Ryan," the guy answered. He cocked his head towards the girl in his arms, "This is my girlfriend, Whitney. Cal is… er… was… her cousin."

"Did Cal have a last name?" Cox asked.

"Bloch," Ryan told him, rubbing Whitney's back, "Calvin Bloch."

"And where was Cal from?"

"Iowa," Ryan responded. He gave a slight shrug, "It might have been Sabula. I think."

"Iowa will do for now," Cox said. He reached up and thumbed his walkie to life, "Dispatch, I need you to make some calls. Try to get Cal Bloch's family on the line. Definitely from Iowa, possibly from Sabula. Also, what's the twenty on that back up."

"Ten-Four, Sarge," came the staticky reply, "Additional units are en route and should be there in five." Cox cleared his throat.

"We're gonna need to transport you down to the station so we can call your families. We're gonna need to hold you for a little

157

while so we can ask you all some questions. In the meantime, when my guys get here, we're gonna survey the scene."

Ryan nodded just as the red and blue flashing lights came barreling up the dirt road towards them. Cox squatted down beside Mindy and put his hand on her arm. Mindy shook her head.

"I can't leave yet," she protested, "I have to find my boyfriend."

"Mindy," Cox said, lowering the tone of his voice, "There's nothing you can do here. I assure you, we'll scour the premises. If he's here, we'll find him. I promise."

"But…" Mindy started. Cox held up his free hand and gave Mindy's arm a gentle but firm squeeze.

"No buts," he told Mindy, "You've clearly had a hell of a time out here. Go back to the station with your friends and get some rest. We'll talk soon."

Mindy nodded but her eyes remained cold, lifeless, and dead. Cox helped her to her feet and motioning to the others, he walked them towards the squad cars.

He knew he was in for a long night.

Downtown

"I'm afraid I have some bad news for you," Cox said, "You may want to sit down."

After being at the police station for what felt like a week and a half, the Westfield Survivors, as they would come to be known in the newspapers for the next several months, were now seated in the small confines of the briefing room. Cox's face was pallid and his face looked as though he had just seen all the world's horrors laid out before him. In truth, he kind of had, at least by Westfield's standards. A quadruple homicide was, in fact, the most gruesome crime scene he had been a part of in quite some time. Cox wiped the perspiration from his upper lip and took a deep breath.

"After you were escorted from the premises, my deputies found the bodies of your friends," he started. He saw the tears welling up in the survivor's eyes and he took a drink of his coffee before he continued, "At least, we assume they were your friends. It's going to be some time before we get a positive identification on that."

As dental records would later prove, the Marquette County Sheriff's department had, indeed, found the bodies of Coral and Kevin in the woods surrounding the blast radius of the abandoned camper. At the present time, the bodies didn't exactly resemble the campers as they had existed in their original incarnation. One of the officers, whom Cox had already personally reprimanded, had put it best when he said they looked like "week old charcoal briquettes."

"What about Cal?" Whitney asked in a small, cracking voice. Cox cleared his throat and laced his fingers together on the table.

"Cal's body was among those found," He informed them, "And that's where the story takes a turn for the worse."

A short bark of laughter escaped Mindy's throat. She slapped her hand over her mouth when everyone in the room looked at her. She shook her head and cleared her throat.

"I'm sorry," She said, "I just find it hard to believe that this could get even worse."

"I understand," Cox nodded, "But I assure you, it can."

According to Cox, dispatch had gotten Cal's home address after contacting Whitney's mother. The dispatcher proceeded to call the Sabula Police Department who, in turn, had sent a uniform to the home of the deceased so as to get in contact with his next of kin. After a period of time knocking on the door, the officers had entered the premises.

"The officer's reported a foul odor coming from within the premises," Cox explained, "When they got inside, they located the remains of Cal's mother and father, both deceased."

"What happened?" Whitney squeaked before turning to bury her face in Ryan's shoulder. Ryan pulled her close.

"According to reports from the neighbors, on Wednesday evening Cal and his parents had an argument when Cal had been up for a disciplinary action from school. He had apparently made some violent verbal comments about a few teachers. He was facing expulsion. Early on Thursday morning, Cal was witnessed leaving the premises in a hurry and, while we are still investigating this matter with cooperation from the Sebula PD, we presume that was when he headed for your house, Whitney," Cox stated. He unlaced his hands and set them on the table before him with the palms up towards the ceiling, "Which seems to make this a pretty open and shut case."

Whitney nodded against Ryan's shoulder. Cox took a deep breath and stood from his chair behind the table. He stood awkwardly, looking at the group before him for a moment, before he walked to the briefing room door and opened it.

"You folks are free to go," Cox said, "No rush. Take all the time you need."

Mindy waited a moment before she stood from her seat and followed Cox out into the hallway. She turned to that Cox was already halfway down the white tiled hall and she jogged to catch up with him.

"Sheriff," She called. Cox, who was on his way back to his office for an aspirin and a glass of whiskey, turned around at the sound of Mindy's voice. He wiped his hand down his face and raised his eyebrows as Mindy stepped up to stand in front of him.

"What can I do for you, ma'am?"

"Call me Mindy, please," she replied. She glanced over her shoulder to make sure that the others were still in the conference room, out of ear shot, before she continued, "I need to know what happened out there?"

"The investigation is ongoing, ma'a…" Cox started but Mindy shook her head disapprovingly.

"Mindy," she corrected him, "And I'm not asking as a victim or a busybody. I want to know the details. I was out there and I saw most of the aftermath firsthand. I think I'm entitled to know what happened."

"You sure you want to hear this?" Cox asked sullenly. Mindy nodded her head.

"I need to know."

"Cal's body was found in the tree above the clearing," Cox stated, "Though I'm sure you saw that."

"I did," she replied, "Was he killed in the explosion?"

"We're not sure yet, Mindy," Cox told her, "But we can assume as such." He decided not to inform her that, if Cal had been lucky, he had been killed in the explosion. If he hadn't been, then there was a good chance that he was still very much alive and badly burned when the explosion had thrown him skywards and he had probably died a slow and excruciatingly painful death while he bled out after being impaled by the tree branch he had landed on. Cox wouldn't say it out loud, especially not to a civilian, but how Cal died was a minor detail of no importance. Dead was dead and, in this case, it had left Portage Prison with a vacant cell, the taxpayers with a handful of their hard earned money in their hands, and a legal system that wasn't being bogged down by endless court proceedings and paperwork.

162

"Did you find Chris?" Mindy asked. Cox rubbed the bridge of his nose with his fingertips.

"I'm sorry, Mindy," Cox said, "I'm not trying to be rude but, which one was Chris?"

"He wouldn't have been in the explosion," Mindy clarified, "He…may have been in the woods. With a hatchet wound?"

"We did find a male victim in the woods with wounds that appeared to come from a hatchet," Cox said, "He was in the woods on the opposite side of the clearing, at the bottom of a gully. Why do you ask?"

"Just wanted to get some of the facts straight," Mindy stated. She looked down at her feet so Cox didn't see the tears welling up in her eyes, "What about Jonas?"

"We haven't found Jonas' body yet," Cox said. He cleared his throat, "And, depending on where he was when the explosion happened, we might not find his remains."

"I understand," Mindy said, choking back a sob. Cox stood uncomfortable, watching Mindy before him. He reached out a hand and placed it on her shoulder.

"We'll do everything we can to get you the closure you need," he said. Mindy nodded. There was a beat of silence, "Any more questions?"

"I think that just about does it," Mindy said. She wiped her eyes and then extended a hand to Cox, "Thank you for all your help."

"You're welcome. You take care of yourself, Mindy," Cox said, shaking her hand, "And make sure your friends do the same."

"We will."

Thirty minutes later, the survivors were all standing on the police station parking lot between Mindy's SUV and Garrett's Jeep. The Westfield Police Department had graciously taken the liberty of fixing the flat tires.

"Do you mind if we catch a ride home with you, Mindy?" Whitney asked.

"What about your Explorer, Ryan?" Mindy asked.

"The cops need to hold on to it for evidence," Ryan said, "But I think it's time for a new set of wheels anyway."

Mindy didn't ask any follow up questions. She knew full well that, even if the police had handed Ryan the keys to the car, he didn't want to drive home in the same car that he had been sharing with a killer just a couple days earlier. Especially when Cal had tried to murder him in the backseat. The gouge in the back door from where the machete had struck would only serve as a reminder of how close he had come to his own demise every time he looked at it. She nodded her head and motioned for the two of them to get in the car. She turned her attention to Garrett.

"You okay, buddy?" She asked him. Garrett pulled out a cigarette and placed it between his lips.

"I'mma be awright, Dee," he drawled, "'S jes' gon' take s'm gittin' use'ta."

"That it will," she said with a sigh. She moved in to give him a hug.

"Yer man, Joe-nass, wouldn'a liked th't much," He said. Mindy smiled.

"A couple of days ago, I would've agreed with you," She replied, feeling a tear trickle down the side of her face, "But I think, at this point, he wouldn't have minded too much."

"See ya'soon, Dee," Garrett said, releasing Mindy from his arms and climbing into his Jeep. He took a second to pause and light his cigarette before he fired up the engine and pulled out of the lot. Mindy waved as he drove off and Mindy watched his car as it slowly disappeared down the road. Once the car was out of sight, Mindy's eyes lingered on the tops of the trees in the distance, watching them rustle in the breeze out on Bear Paw Road. She closed her eyes.

Then, slowly, she walked back to her SUV, and started the trip back home.

The Last Hurrah

A few months later, just as the hustle and bustle was finally beginning to die down and life had started its slow ascent back to some semblance of normalcy, Mindy was just getting ready to leave work for the day when her phone rang. She dug through her purse and glanced at the caller ID before answering. It was Ryan.

"Mindy, you're never going to believe this," Ryan said, bypassing any form of salutation and cutting directly to the chase, "Come across the street." Mindy started to ask what he was talking about, but Ryan had already hung up the phone. She shrugged her shoulders and, picking up her purse and lunch box, she walked out the front door of the bank, crossed the parking lot and got behind the wheel of her car. She pulled out of the lot onto the highway and turned into the parking lot for the strip mall across the street. She scanned the parking lots until she saw Ryan and Whitney standing beside Ryan's new ride. She pulled into the spot next to them, put the car in park and stepped out.

"What the hell is going on?" She asked, thumbing the lock button on her key fob. Ryan didn't respond. He grabbed her by the arm and pulled her across the parking lot and the through the front door of the bookstore.

Just inside the front doors, Ryan stopped and thrust a hand out, motioning towards the table of new release before them. No further explanation was needed. Ryan let go of Mindy's arm and she took a step forward. Looking down at the tableful of books, she reached out her hand and ran her fingertips over the glossy book cover before her. She picked a copy up, reading the title, *The Curbside Novelist*, before turning it over. A bittersweet smile crossed her face as a warm tear welled up in her eye, rolled down her cheek, and dripped off her face, landing with a tiny splash on the black and white picture of Jonas Reilly's smiling face.

She knew that somewhere, between the moon and the stars, Jonas was finally assured that he was worth a damn.

Made in the USA
Middletown, DE
21 August 2024

59557874R00103